NOT

REALLY

DEAD

A Tess Winnett
Novella

LESLIE WOLFE

PRAISE FOR *NOT REALLY DEAD*

"It has been a while since I enjoyed a book this much."

"I would definitely recommend this book/series to anyone that loves crime novels!"

"It's fast moving, good story and had no clue who did it until the very end. A true "who dunnit"."

"This is an awesome read! Definitely keeps you interested, couldn't put it down! A definite must read"

"Once I started reading, I had to finish right away. The book is written to pull you in and keep you reading...until you know! Great read, as always!"

"As with all the Tess Winnett books, this one kept me riveted right up until the end. Now I cannot wait for the next installment."

"For me, this book was excellent, suspenseful, and entertaining. Highly recommend."

"Great female characters. Fantastic research. This whole series is wonderful. Please keep it up."

PRAISE FOR LESLIE WOLFE

"This is my first book I have read from this author, but I am looking forward to reading more."

"I have read many books by Ms Wolfe in the Tess Winnett series. This has quickly become my favorite series. I'm so glad I was recommended by Amazon. If you are looking for a new series read anything by Leslie Wolfe."

"Nothing beats reading a Leslie Wolfe book to get your blood pumping. They are just that good."

BOOKS BY LESLIE WOLFE

STANDALONE TITLES

A Beautiful Couple
The Surgeon
The Girl You Killed
The Hospital
If I Go Missing
Stories Untold
Love, Lies and Murder

TESS WINNETT SERIES

Dawn Girl
The Watson Girl
Glimpse of Death
Taker of Lives
Not Really Dead
Girl With A Rose
Mile High Death
The Girl They Took
The Girl Hunter

DETECTIVE KAY SHARP SERIES

The Girl From Silent Lake
Beneath Blackwater River
The Angel Creek Girls
The Girl on Wildfire Ridge
Missing Girl at Frozen Falls

BAXTER & HOLT SERIES

Las Vegas Girl
Casino Girl
Las Vegas Crime

ALEX HOFFMANN SERIES

Executive
Devil's Move
The Backup Asset
The Ghost Pattern
Operation Sunset

For the complete list of books in all available formats, visit:
Amazon.com/LeslieWolfe

NOT REALLY DEAD

A Tess Winnett Novella

LESLIE WOLFE

ⅠⅠ ITALICS

Italics Publishing Inc.

Edited by Joni Wilson and Susan Barnes.
Cover and interior design by Sam Roman.

ACKNOWLEDGMENT

A special thank you to Mark Freyberg, my New York City authority for all matters legal. Mark's command of the law and passion for deciphering its intricacies translates into zero unanswered questions for this author. He's a true legal oracle and a wonderful friend.

Chapter 1

The touch of his warm fingers still sent shivers through her body, although she felt a knot in her throat, threatening tears and a ruined end to the evening. She tried to paste a smile on her face and squeezed his hand, hoping he wouldn't sense how sad she really felt.

"Danielle, we talked about this," he whispered, while the limo took the exit heading for her house.

She nodded, not trusting her voice enough to say anything.

He wrapped his arm around her shoulders, and somehow that made things a little better. She craved his presence like an insatiable addict, wanted to share every waking moment with him and fall asleep in his arms at the end of each day. She'd fallen for him hard, beyond repair, beyond any of her wildest dreams.

And she was being unreasonable. She blinked away the tears, willing herself to remember Stephen belonged to her; they were engaged, soon to be married, and the engagement ring on her finger stood testimony to that. She counted the days until the wedding, set for October 19.

Set by others, not by them.

The most important date of her life had been chosen after several days of arguing and meetings and negotiations among Stephen's father, his campaign manager, and his countless advisors, publicists, and media experts.

Her future father-in-law was running for president, in one of the most heated races for the White House in the history of the United States.

The moment Stephen had proposed to her, after a fabulous

dinner followed by champagne served in tall flutes on a gold tray, her life had started spinning out of control.

She'd known who she was saying yes to. The love of her life, true, but also a man who was going to be at the center of media attention for the next few months, or even years, if his father won.

Secretly, she hoped he'd lose. She wanted to marry Stephen the lawyer, the one overwhelmed by student loan debt just like her, not the president's son with everything that statement entailed. Somewhere between the day she met Stephen and the day he proposed, his father had emerged from the ranks of anonymity and shot all the way into earning a Democratic nomination almost overnight.

She wanted their old life back; but what she wanted no longer mattered that much. Except for Stephen... she could still marry him, but even that came at a cost.

She'd known every inch of her background would be examined under a magnifying glass by investigators who wanted to dig up any speck of dirt before it could cause real problems for the man they already called "Mr. President" in private. She cringed when she recalled her high school flings, her first frat party, the first time she drank a little too much; they would find out about it, in every sordid little detail. Her fiancé would read about all that in a report.

She'd known that their schedule would be set by others, and the moments alone with Stephen would become treasured gems, difficult to find but even more gratifying as their scarcity increased their value.

She'd known all that and she'd said yes, with a swelling heart full of love and a slightly trembling voice.

Yet she had no reason to feel so sad, so needy, just because he had to leave her side a few nights a week to help with his father's campaign efforts. The man sitting by her side on the leather backseat of that limo was every woman's dream and deserved better than a clingy, tearful drama queen.

"Danielle," he whispered, then kissed her hand, their fingers intertwined, their heads close together.

"Yes, I know you have to leave. I just wish you could spend the night with me, that's all," she pleaded, unshed tears coloring her voice, untrue to her own commitment to show him the support he deserved. "Tonight, more than ever."

"Not tonight, my love," he replied, searching her eyes with a worried glance. "I'm really sorry, I can't. I have that early morning flight with everyone on the team. But tomorrow, when I get back, I'm coming straight here."

The driver pulled up at the curb in front of her house, the second on a small Palm Beach street tucked behind the parking lot of a bar, one of those old-style places with the owner's living quarters on the second floor.

"Can you forgive me?" Stephen asked, his voice only a hint louder, getting ready to say goodbye.

She nodded again, then gently pulled her hand out of his, regretful when their fingers parted. She wanted those fingers to rip the clothes off her body and explore every inch of her skin, while she begged for mercy.

The driver held the door for her, waiting patiently. She turned toward Stephen, and he didn't hesitate. He cradled her face in his hands and pressed his lips against hers, tasting her, building a sense of urgency inside her that made her entire being shiver with desire.

Then he let go.

She pulled away reluctantly but managed a smile, then

walked the short distance to her door and unlocked it. She turned toward the car one more time, smiled and waved, and saw Stephen waving back.

The limo driver closed the door and took his place behind the wheel.

By the time she reached the living room window and looked outside, the limo was gone.

Silence and a sense of dread, of inexplicable angst, overwhelmed her. The house she'd decorated with so much enjoyment seemed cold and unwelcoming, as if shadows were lurking in every corner, ready to pounce.

She shrugged off her fears and checked the thermostat. It was the south of Florida, but she didn't care. If it felt cold, she needed heat. She switched it to heating and added a few degrees on the setting, then rubbed her hands together to warm them.

She poured herself a glass of red wine, took a sip, but didn't feel any of the warmth she was hoping for. Instead, the wine seemed sour and cold. Disappointed, she abandoned the glass on the counter and took out her phone, searching for some music to play, to lift her spirit. Between browsing playlists, she texted Stephen, "Miss you already."

A chime came immediately after. "Me too. Sweet dreams, baby."

Then Adele's vibrant voice broke the silence, sharing rumors with anyone who wanted to listen, an older song Danielle loved since her heydays in high school.

Better.

The thought of a shower seemed appealing, the warmth from the water jets promising to soothe her and deliver a good night's sleep in the bed that now seemed too large for only her. She went back into the living room and unbuttoned the turquoise blouse that matched her eyes, then slid off the tight, black pencil skirt. Both items landed on a nearby chair, followed quickly by her lacy underwear. She slipped on a sateen robe she'd dropped on the couch that morning and started walking toward the bathroom, the distance too short to be worth tying the sash around her waist.

She never made it that far.

She sensed him before she saw him, a rise in the hairs on the back of her neck, primal fear unfurling in her gut, a scream emerging from her throat that never reached her lips. The unfamiliar smell of a stranger, the barely audible sound of approaching footfalls muffled by the music, a sense of impending doom urging her to run for her life.

Then she felt his hands on her body, grabbing her and slamming her down to the floor so hard it knocked the air out of her lungs. She thrashed, kicking and hitting the man as best as she could, but her gasping efforts only brought a grin to his face. She managed to push herself away from him a little, sliding on the hardwood floor, and started to get up, but he caught her with one hand, while with the other he pulled out a knife, the 6-inch blade reflecting the lights coming from the chandelier. He seized her neck and started squeezing, slowly, his face closer to her inch by inch, the coldness of the blade burning her skin.

Darkness drew closer as his fingers tightened around her neck. She gasped, desperate for air, while thoughts whirled through her head. Stephen... she'd never see him again.

She was going to die.

"Not yet," the man hissed, then cackled loudly after licking his lips, his pupils dilated with loaded anticipation. "You and I are not done yet." He let go of her throat and drove his hand lower. "I promise you'll love it."

She drew gasps of air, filling her lungs over and over again, desperately thinking of a way out. She lunged for the door but felt the blade slicing against her side and hesitated. The man raised his hand, and the blow came down hard across her face, sending her tumbling across the floor, seeing stars.

Everything turned dark.

Chapter 2

Tess entered the federal building at two minutes after eight, rushing up the stairs with a tall coffee in one hand and her briefcase in the other. Her scramble soon took its toll in the form of a rebel coffee drop that escaped the confines of the cup lid and stained the sleeve of her starched, white shirt, bringing a groan of frustration to her lips.

She placed the paper cup on her desk and dropped the briefcase on her chair, then noticed a yellow Post-it note affixed to her monitor. "Come see me ASAP," the note read, lacking a signature, but only one person in the building had the nasty habit of leaving handwritten sticky notes instead of using the phone, like the rest of the world did.

Her boss, Special Agent in Charge Pearson.

"Ugh," she groaned again, not eager to face him. She had a good idea what the invitation was about. She'd just closed a case, but she knew he wasn't calling her in to congratulate her.

She stepped into the hallway and checked to see if the light was on in his office, then groaned again and started walking down the hall. A moment later, she rushed back, picked up her coffee, then resumed the earlier course toward her boss's office.

The door was open, but she knocked twice against the doorframe and waited. Pearson's eyes stayed riveted on a couple of forms he was perusing, on occasion making scribbled notes on the edges of the paper. She recognized her signature at the bottom of one form and repressed a sigh.

She must've screwed up the paperwork again.

Pearson gave no sign he was aware of her presence, but she wasn't that easily fooled. If she would've knocked again, he would've given her a long stare. He was quite predictable, at least to her.

But then again, most people were. That was the norm for behavioral analysts.

She started studying the man, lacking anything else to do and unwilling to let her mind wander further away. She could tell he'd been preoccupied that morning, because he'd thrown his jacket sideways across a chair, instead of draping it on the chair's back to keep it from wrinkling. He was also in a sour mood, because he kept rapping his fingertips against the desk's walnut finish in an irritating, impatient rhythm, and every now and then he ran his chubby hand across his shiny scalp, as if he still had hair. If he had, he'd probably be pulling it right now.

Tess frowned, a little worried, and shifted her weight from one foot to the other. She wondered exactly what was causing those deep trenches ridging Pearson's brow.

Without a word and without looking at her, he waved her in, leisurely pointing at the chair in front of his desk. She obliged quietly and waited, coffee cup still in hand.

SAC Pearson let the papers fall from his hand and leaned back in his chair.

"You closed the Pacheco case," he said, speaking slowly, his concern transparent.

No, he hadn't called her in to congratulate her.

She nodded. "Yes, I did."

"By shooting the unsub as he fled the scene," Pearson added calmly. "In the back."

"Um, yes, sir. But this particular unknown subject—"

"There were civilians present. Twenty-three, to be exact, including four children." He looked straight at her, his gaze loaded with disappointment and frustration. "Some of these people stated they heard the bullet whistling by as it passed within inches of their heads."

"No one was hurt except the unsub," she reacted, but quickly fell quiet when Pearson glared at her.

"There will be a formal review," he added, then removed his thick-rimmed glasses and rubbed the root of his nose between his left thumb and index finger. "You always do this, Winnett. You just can't help yourself, can you?"

Silence fell heavy and uncomfortable, filling the room like a toxic gas.

"Do what, exactly?" she eventually asked.

"Screw things up at the end." He picked up the report and read from it for a few seconds, then let it drop again. "What happened at Biscayne and Little River yesterday, Winnett? Why did you pull the trigger?"

She cleared her throat quietly. "Pacheco was making a run for it and was about to catch a departing bus. My car was two blocks away, and we had no one else in pursuit. We would've never caught him again, sir."

"We have procedures for a reason, Winnett. There's no excuse for opening fire on a fleeing suspect in the middle of a crowd."

"It wasn't a crowd, sir. No one was close. And that bastard raped and killed five preteen girls. I wasn't about to let him escape. Under the fleeing felon rule, if it's in the interest of public safety, it's acceptable—"

"You'll have to answer a few questions," he said, running his hand across his forehead as if to stretch the deepening ridges of his furrowed brow. "In front of a formal review board."

"Better than to tell another parent we're too late, sir," she replied steadily, unflinching, almost cold. She knew she was in trouble, yet she didn't feel bad about what had happened.

"Are you sure that's what this was about, Winnett? The victims? Or was it about your case clearance rate that you want to maintain as perfect?"

She repressed a smile. No one else had the enviable, 100 percent clearance rate Pearson was referencing.

"Isn't it the same thing, sir? We're tasked to protect the public, and we're measured against that goal."

SAC Pearson shook his head. "Jeez, Winnett. How close were the nearest civilians?"

"At least a few feet."

"And Pacheco?"

"Thirty yards and opening."

He shook his head again. "Don't let anyone interview you without me present, understand?"

"Yes, sir." She stood silently, waiting, ready to leave the room. Eventually, he pointed at the chair she'd just vacated, and she retook the seat.

"I have a new case for you," he said, pushing a thick file across the desk. "BCI Insurance Services. Fraud and conspiracy to commit."

"Oh."

Her obvious disappointment immediately raised Pearson's eyebrow. "Not fancy enough for you, Winnett?"

"I'm a skilled manhunter, sir. I understand there will be an investigation into the Pacheco shooting, but is there a murder case open that I could be looking into? This," she pointed at the thick file on his desk, "anyone can do. It's just paperwork and analysis."

"You're arrogant, Winnett; and it doesn't suit you," Pearson replied, pushing the file an inch closer to her hand. She withdrew her hand and promptly placed it in her lap as if the proximity of the file burned her skin.

"There's the Word Killer case still open. I believe SA Patto is working that."

"Yes, SA Patto is handling that one."

She scoffed quietly. "Patto has been dancing with this killer for a while now, sir, and nothing. No results."

"Winnett!"

"Please, allow me to look into this case before I lose myself down the rabbit hole of fraudulent health insurance plans."

"Patto's case is exactly that, Winnett, it's Patto's case. We don't yank cases from agents when other agents want a piece of their action. That is not how we work. We're a team."

She stood abruptly and placed her hands on the desk, leaning forward, towering over Pearson, a strategic mistake that she didn't realize she was making. "Did Patto mention the killer is escalating? Did he figure that out yet? Patto's not a profiler."

"I don't want to hear it, Winnett. You have your case assignment, and Patto has his."

"The way the Word Killer is carving on the bodies of his victims, the words he leaves behind written in blood on the walls, he's not going to stop. He's just getting started. Please, sir." She ended her tirade on a more subdued tone, likely to appease the growing anger she discerned in her boss's glare.

"Yeah, you're an excellent behavioral analyst, Winnett. Quantico wants you, Bill McKenzie holds a spot open for you—yours when you want it. Why are you still here?"

"Oh," she reacted, surprised to hear he knew about it. "I don't feel I'm ready for that kind of action, not yet."

"Is that the real reason? Or is it the fact that the Behavioral Analysis Unit works as a team and only as a team?"

Her phone started to vibrate, and she threw the screen a fleeting look before sending the call to voicemail. It was Cat. He never called so early in the morning. He almost never called.

Frowning, she looked at Pearson, eager to leave, glad to leave his question unanswered.

"Thankfully, Florida doesn't have nearly enough blood-lusting killers to keep you satisfied, Winnett. So BCI Insurance it is, if you choose to stay here, under my command."

The threat was unveiled and unmistakable, and yet she didn't stop pleading.

"But you have one blood-lusting predator out there, the Word Killer. He's about to strike again, if he hasn't already, and Patto doesn't even know about it."

Pearson stood in one abrupt move and grabbed the thick file, lifting it in the air. Then he slammed it on the desk with a loud noise.

"BCI Insurance, Winnett. Or else."

They locked eyes for a long moment, then she lowered hers while she picked up the file, defeated. If she still wanted a job, she needed to learn to take orders.

"You are dismissed," Pearson said, after she'd already turned to leave.

Chapter 3

As soon as Tess left Pearson's office, she took out her phone, frowning as she retrieved Cat's voicemail. She couldn't think of another time he'd left her a message, not in the twelve years she'd known him, since he'd saved her life and became the closest thing she'd had to a father. Cat was stuck in his ways like most people his age, refusing to use all the functions of a cell phone, and for him to break that pattern of behavior was enough reason for concern.

She tapped the screen and put the phone to her ear, listening intently.

"Sorry to bother you at work, kiddo," Cat had said in a guarded whisper, panting a little as if he'd climbed a flight of stairs faster than usual. "Um, if you could come by this morning, I'd appreciate it." He'd paused for a moment, as if unsure what to say next. "Please," he'd added, then hung up.

Not good.

She didn't even pass by her desk to get rid of the BCI file; instead, she patted her pants pocket to make sure she had her car keys and rushed to the parking lot and, within minutes, she was burning rubber leaving the area. When she turned the corner, she switched on the flashing lights and the siren and started weaving through traffic as fast as she could.

When she pulled up in front of the Media Luna Bar and Grill, she cut the noise, but she was going too fast, and her SUV's wheels threw gravel high in the air, making a grinding sound as the car came to a stop. The "Open" neon sign was off, quite normal for nine in the morning, and only Cat's Jeep was visible, parked in its usual spot, left of the building, leaving all the front places for the customers.

She climbed out of her vehicle, carefully looking around for any sign of trouble, resisting the urge to pull out her weapon. After all, Cat hadn't said anything was wrong; he'd just asked her to come by. If she showed up with her gun drawn, he'd probably never dare to call her again.

She heard a whistle coming from the second floor and looked up. Cat's head popped out through an open window, his finger touching his lips in a plea for silence. She nodded, and he beckoned her upstairs, then disappeared from view.

She took the side stairs to the apartment, struggling to ignore the wave of memories that overwhelmed her the moment she opened the door. She breathed deeply and focused; he hadn't called her over for something that had happened almost twelve years ago; she could bet good money on that.

He met her in the hallway of the small apartment, his finger back at his lips, urging silence. She hadn't seen him in a while, and these days, a while, any length of time really, seemed to make her previously ageless friend appear a little bit older. He still wore his signature Hawaiian shirt, unbuttoned at the first two or three buttonholes, enough to allow a peek of the tiger tattoo, now barely visible, matted and discolored, that had brought him the nickname he allowed very few to use. His hair, almost entirely white, still touched his shoulders in loose waves but was thinned out, and his forehead had gained a few inches in height. His face was still tan and his eyes sharper than ever, but he looked tired, drawn.

Cat was getting old.

That simple statement brought tears to her eyes. Silently, she vowed she'd find a way to come by more often, maybe help at the bar a few nights a week.

He leaned down and put a quick smooch on her cheek, grabbed her hand and led her into the bedroom. She followed, curious and surprised, but when she saw the figure lying between the sheets she gasped, a quick and loud intake of air before she covered her mouth with her hand.

Frozen in place and trembling under the wave of unrelenting memories, she studied the young woman resting under the white down duvet on Cat's bed. She was young, twenty-two, maybe twenty-three years old. Her face was bruised but clean; Cat must've cleaned the young woman's wounds like he'd done for her ages ago. Dried tears had left streaks on her face. Her hair, auburn-gold and long with bottom lowlights, was tangled in places where blood had dried on it, clumping the strands together. A deep cut ran along her neck, cleaned and patched with Mickey Mouse butterfly Band-Aids.

She shifted in her sleep and started whimpering, but Cat sat in the bedside armchair, grabbed her hand, and began soothing her.

"Shhh... I'm right here, and you're safe. You can sleep now."

It was as if Tess were looking at an image of herself, a ghost from another time.

She closed her eyes for a moment, and the unwanted memories rushed in. She saw herself crawling to the pub's door, bleeding, barely conscious, hurt within an inch of her life. She remembered waking in that bed twelve years ago, patched up, cleaned, her body screaming with pain. She'd found Cat by her side, saying the same things, doing the same things he was doing now for this young woman. She vividly relived the pain, the fear, the anger, as if she were going through it all over again. She recalled healing slowly, nurtured back to life by a kind stranger, a man who'd saved her life and asked for nothing in return.

Tears quietly rolled down her face; she couldn't hold them back anymore. She'd kept them bottled up for so many years, and finally they could flow freely, the floodgates now open. When she dared, she opened her eyes and looked at Cat.

"Again?" she asked, with a sad smile on her lips.

"I'm sorry, kiddo... I didn't know what else to do," he whispered.

She shook her head and wiped her tears away with the back of her hand. He had no reason to apologize. "It's all right." She slowly approached the bed, afraid the floors might creak, and the young woman would startle from her sleep.

"What happened to her?"

He shrugged, while deep ridges marked his brow.

"If I could get my hands on this son of a bitch, I'd rip his insides out and strangle him with them until he stopped drawing breath."

"Tell me what happened," Tess said, keeping her voice low. She crouched next to Cat's armchair, her eyes on the same level with his. "Step by step."

"I was about to close the place for the night," he said, then stopped his account when the girl whimpered again. She was dreaming, probably screaming in her sleep. "A couple of regulars were passed out at the tables, and I was getting ready to call them a cab, you know."

She nodded encouragingly. "Keep going."

"Then I heard someone banging on the door but didn't see anyone, so I went outside and found her, bleeding. I brought her in."

"What was she wearing?"

He gently let go of the young woman's hand and sighed as

he stood up from the armchair with some difficulty. "I knew you were going to ask me that, so I packed it in a Ziploc bag."

He went into the small bathroom and returned with a plastic bag holding a mauve, silky garment, profusely stained with blood. "Just this, a fancy robe, I guess."

"No underwear?"

He lowered his eyes. "No." His jaws clenched and his fists too. "She was, um, there was blood... I could kill him with my bare hands—"

She touched his shoulder, then squeezed it gently. "I get it, Cat. Trust me, I do."

"Now I understand why you do what you do for a living. Someone's got to put these monsters down. Promise me you'll get this son of a bitch, just like you nailed that other bastard."

"I'll do my best, Cat."

"I'm proud of you, you know? What you do... It must be terrible to see this every day, people like this, hurt, tortured, killed." He slowly paced the room, wringing his hands. "What the hell ever happened to people, huh? It's like 'Nam out there, in the streets."

She walked over to him and grabbed his hands in hers. "I have to call it in, Cat. She needs a hospital."

"No," he reacted, his whisper filled with intensity. "She made me swear I wouldn't." He searched her eyes, pleading. "Just like you did."

Damn... another unwanted memory. Cat had taken a big chance caring for her on his own. Failure to report the crime could've got him charged with a felony; worst-case scenario, he could've done serious time as an accessory after the fact. Yet he'd done it all for her, so she could still have a life and a career with the FBI unmarred by the stigma of sexual assault. He was willing to do it again.

"Did she say why we can't call it in?"

He shook his head once, staring into thin air. "There will be time for that later, when she wakes up."

She walked over to the window, thinking. "Did she mention anything about her attacker?"

"No."

"Did she say anything else? Her name, maybe?"

"Danielle," he replied after a split second's hesitation. "She said her name is Danielle"

Chapter 4

Tess leaned her forehead against the cold window, looking at the gloomy winter sky and wondering what she should do. Her law enforcement training demanded that Danielle file a formal complaint and go to the hospital for a rape kit, in the hope that the attacker had left behind his DNA. But her own memories were still raw after all those years; she remembered how terrified she'd been about her life being forever marked by the four-letter word that brought undue shame to the victims.

Either way, on or off the record, she wasn't going to let that bastard walk.

Danielle whimpered in her sleep, then woke abruptly, sitting anxiously, pulse racing, ready to run. She seemed oddly familiar, like someone Tess might've seen in traffic recently or on TV.

"It's okay, you're safe here," Cat said, looking straight at her with a kind smile.

"Uh-huh," she whispered, out of breath. She looked around the room, panicked, and saw Tess; her pupils dilated, and she withdrew farther away on the bed, as if Tess was going to hurt her.

"I'm here to help," Tess said, speaking as gently as she could. She wasn't used to dealing with live victims, but she understood what the girl must've felt.

"Who are you?" she asked, nervously licking her dry lips.

"She's a good friend, someone you can trust," Cat replied, "I called her."

"Why?" the girl asked, looking at Tess with increasing fear.

"Danielle, I'm a federal agent," Tess said.

The girl instantly burst into heart-wrenching wails. "You promised," she said, looking at Cat. "You swore to me," she added, trying to get out of the bed, wincing in pain with every move.

Cat looked at Tess with an unspoken plea in his eyes.

"I'm not here in any official capacity," Tess said, frowning a little when she noticed how ineffective her statement had been. Danielle's tears flowed in streaks down her bruised face, her shoulders heaving with every sobbing breath she took.

Tess approached the bed and slowly sat on its edge, careful not to cause her any additional pain. "Listen, I will not report this, unless you want me to," she said, holding the girl's hand with both hers. "No one will know."

Danielle looked at her with a glimmer of hope in her eyes. "You promise?"

"I swear," Tess replied with a tiny smile, fighting back her own tears. "Cat and I will keep you safe. I'll get the man who did this to you."

She sniffled and nodded a couple of times. "Thank you," she whispered.

"But I need you to cooperate with me," Tess added. "First priority is your health. I need to know how badly you're hurt, and if you need a hospital."

Panic returned in full force in the girl's round eyes. "No, no, please. No hospital."

Tess nodded, then glanced at Cat quickly.

"Okay, we'll try," she conceded. "May I touch you?" she asked, leaning forward a little.

Danielle whispered, "Yes."

Tess traced the cut on her neck to the place where it disappeared in her thick hair.

"How did this happen?"

She swallowed hard. "He… slammed me down, and I hit something." A fresh tear rolled down her cheek. "The coffee table, maybe. I don't remember."

"You could have a concussion," Tess said, feeling more and more uneasy with Danielle's decision to avoid the hospital.

"I checked her pupillary response in both eyes," Cat said. "She's not throwing up, and she's not dizzy, so I think we're good." His grin widened a little when he noticed Tess's doubtful look. "I was a medic in 'Nam, in case you forgot."

"That was a long time ago," Tess replied.

"Human skulls were the same back then as they are today. I'm sure she'll be fine."

Tess turned to look at Danielle again. The young woman avoided her scrutiny.

"How about the rest of you?" she asked, lowering her voice a little.

"I think it's time to go downstairs and fix some soup," Cat said as he walked out of the room, closing the door behind him. Danielle followed his departure with wary eyes, then glanced briefly at Tess, her fear renewed.

Tess waited for the door to close and looked at Danielle for a moment.

"A few years ago, I was lying in this bed, going through the same hell as you are now. Believe it or not, I'm on your side."

She noticed the girl's apprehension wane a little.

"Work with me, please," Tess insisted.

"Okay," she whispered.

"Why won't you let me call this in?"

Danielle stared at Tess for a moment, as if weighing how much she could be trusted. "Because I'm about to marry

Stephen Ross, Larry Ross's son."

"Oh," Tess reacted, a frown deepening on her brow. That's why she seemed familiar; Tess must've seen her on the news.

Danielle's relationship to the presidential candidate complicated things in a dramatic way. If any of it ever got out, Tess would lose her job on the spot, considering the political implications and her current popularity with the state governor. Lately, he'd called Pearson and complained about every case she'd worked on, especially when she'd bothered Miami's rich and influential with her uncomfortable questions and direct mannerisms.

What were the chances of the Secret Service figuring out what had happened and starting to look into the case? What were the chances that the best of Tess and Cat's intentions would blow up in their faces, landing them both in jail?

Pretty solid, Tess thought. More reasons to do this by the book than off the book.

On the other hand, she cringed when she thought of what the media would do if they ever found out about the assault, and how the opposing candidate would use this poor girl's misfortune to twist things to his advantage.

Screw them… all of them.

Even if her career was at stake, the choice was an easy one, because it wasn't really that much of a choice.

"Your secret's safe with me," she said. "Now, tell me how you feel, so we make sure you'll be all right. Are you bleeding?" Tess asked quietly.

"N—no, I don't think so. It hurts, but…"

"Any other cuts, bruises, anything I should see?"

Her chin trembled with the threat of tears. "He… cut me, on my back. He pinned me down and kept cutting, laughing when

I screamed."

Tess closed her eyes for a brief moment. "I'm so sorry, Danielle," she said, giving the girl's hand a quick squeeze. "I need to see that."

She nodded, subdued, blood leaving her face as she turned under the duvet. Slowly, with a quiet moan of pain, she lay on her stomach and with a weak hand gesture invited Tess to take a look.

Tess slowly pulled down the covers, observing carefully all the details she knew Doc Rizza would look for. There were no ligature marks on her ankles, but her legs were bruised badly. There were several superficial cuts and scrapes, probably from her thrashing and fighting the attacker. Tess lifted the old, white T-shirt Cat had given Danielle and exposed her lower back. A rectangular bandage covered a section above her left buttock, and she gently peeled it off. Several cuts, about 3 inches each, had been cleaned and bandaged by Cat, but she could still make out what the unsub had carved into her body.

One number, one letter: 3D. Two characters, nine cuts, their edges always crossing.

Her breath caught, realizing where she'd seen it before. The Word Killer had carved similar symbols on his other victims' bodies, and the coroner had ruled the carvings had been performed antemortem, while the victims were still alive. It was initially ruled as a form of torture, but later, even that not-so-sharp SA Patto had figured out the carvings had to have a meaning.

As for figuring out what the symbols meant, no such luck yet.

One thought kept whirling in Tess's mind, a pesky little fact she couldn't afford to ignore. The Word Killer never left any survivors. Why was Danielle still alive?

"May I take a few photos of your injuries?" Tess asked. "I promise your face won't show."

"Uh-huh," the girl replied, promptly burying her face deeper into the pillow and covering what was still visible of her face with her hand. One of her fingernails was badly torn, and two others were snapped, as if only the tips had broken when she'd scratched her assailant. Tess wondered if she'd be able to take scrapings from underneath her fingernails, like she'd seen Doc Rizza do so many times.

One thing at a time, she reminded herself, taking photos with her phone camera.

"Good," Tess announced, sliding the phone back into her pocket. "Now, let's walk through everything you remember."

The girl turned around and propped herself higher on the pillows. "I don't know... It happened so quickly."

"What did he look like?"

"White," she said, after thinking for a moment. "Under thirty, I think. With mean eyes."

"Any tattoos, anything distinctive you might have noticed?"

She shook her head and lowered her eyes, disappointed. "He struck me, and I fell. I couldn't see much."

"Did he say anything?"

Danielle looked sideways to hide her tears.

"He kept saying that I'll like it," she whispered on a long, shattered breath that ended in a sob. "That I'll want more, and that I'll never forget him." Her shoulders heaved with sobs. "I never will, will I?"

Tess took her hand and squeezed it. "No, you never will," she replied. Danielle looked at her, surprised. "But soon, after we've put him away and you know he's never going to hurt you again, you'll find some peace."

Silence fell heavy between them, and Tess let it play, unwilling to say anything else. She'd already said enough. She focused on what details she recalled from the casual examination of the Word Killer file. What did those symbols mean?

"He called me Delilah," Danielle said. "I kept saying my name was Danielle, thinking he might've made a mistake. But he kept calling me Delilah."

Tess pulled out her phone and typed a quick text to Donovan.

"Please send me the entire Word Killer file and all the attachments, including crime scene photos and any other evidence," her message said.

"Isn't that Patto's case?" the reply came promptly. "Keep this on the DL?"

She replied by sending him a thumbs-up emoticon, then turned to Danielle.

"How did you get away?"

She wiped away her tears with trembling fingers. "After he... finished with me, I tried to run, but he caught me. He hit me really hard, and I blacked out on the floor. When I came to, I heard him talking to himself in the living room and laughing like a crazy man, so I snuck out."

Tess sprung to her feet. "He was still in your house when you left?"

"Y—yes," she replied, gathering the duvet around her thin, shaking body as if it could offer her protection. "Why?"

Tess opened the door, ready to rush downstairs, but Cat was slowly climbing the stairs, careful not to spill the cup of steaming soup.

"Cat, we have a serious problem," Tess announced. "The

bastard knows she got away alive."

Cat put the bowl of soup on the night table, then lifted his shirt, pointing at the .45 Colt 1911 tucked in his belt.

"I'll be ready for him."

She patted him on the shoulder, shaking her head a little to loosen the knot in her throat. Her hero, ready to die for a stranger. She turned to the girl, now pale as the white duvet wrapped around her body.

"Danielle, where do you live?"

Chapter 5

Tess walked to Danielle's house, wearing a black hoodie she'd borrowed from Cat and a pair of oversized shades she kept in her SUV for stakeouts, on the odd chance the unsub was still at the scene or watching the house. Dressed like that and letting a few of her blonde locks escape the hood, she hoped the unsub, if he was indeed watching, could mistake her for Danielle and take the bait, come finish her off. She'd kept her service Glock holstered on her belt, but tucked her smaller backup weapon, a Sig 365, in her right pocket. As she opened the door, she kept her finger on the trigger, ready to fire. As soon as she entered the small house, she pulled out the gun and proceeded to clear it room by room.

When the last room was cleared, she holstered her weapon with a sigh; she'd hoped, against all reason, that she'd find the unsub there, waiting, eager to finish off the girl who got away after having seen his face. Instead, all she found was a crime scene covered in blood.

She'd read about the Word Killer in Mandy Alvarado's case file, his first known victim; he liked to surprise his victims inside their homes and attack them violently, his actions speaking to a sadistic lust killer's profile. The unsub was a man who found enjoyment in the suffering of his victims, in the pain he inflicted without hesitation, unable to obtain sexual gratification in the absence of torture and total control over his victims. The state of Danielle's house supported those assertions.

There were several small scratches on the back-door lock, as if he had fumbled with the lockpick before getting in. Then the unsub must've waited for Danielle in the small hallway that led to the storage closet.

Tess traced Danielle's movements step by step, based on what she'd shared. She'd poured herself some wine but left the glass on the counter. It was right where she'd said it would be. Then she'd taken off her clothes, getting ready for a shower. The garments were scattered on the floor, mixed with debris from a broken chair, at the center of the living room.

But something else caught Tess's eye as she entered the living room. The unsub had started writing on the wall with the victim's blood. Large, streaky letters spelled, "Arrogan," leaving Tess to wonder about the unsub's intended word. Was it arrogant? Or arrogance?

Tess pulled out her phone and scrolled through the digitized case file Donovan had sent to her email, looking for information that could help her better understand the clues left behind by the Word Killer.

His first victim, Mandy Alvarado, a twenty-seven-year-old, divorced, single mother of a two-year-old girl, had been found in a pool of her own blood. Thankfully, her daughter was unharmed, other than having witnessed her mother's murder. The killer had written the word, "Greed" on the victim's wall, and that finding had confused the investigators. What greed? The victim was a single mother, an accountant earning seventy grand a year. Not much greed to be found anywhere.

A second victim, Earlene Burnett, brought another blood-spelled word, "Lust," equally confusing for the twenty-nine-year-old freight pilot with an impeccable record.

Christi Conner, the youngest of the unsub's victims, had died with "Avarice" scribbled on the wall above her head. The affluent socialite had a reputation for generosity, choosing to donate significant amounts of her inheritance to a variety of charities.

The only thing Tess could ascertain from her study was that the unsub had probably wanted to spell "Arrogance" on Danielle's wall; in all prior cases the words were nouns, not adjectives.

Still, she'd met Danielle, and there wasn't an arrogant bone in her body. Noun or adjective, it didn't make sense.

Was it really the Word Killer who'd attacked Danielle? All evidence seemed to point his way, but the carvings, the words written on the walls were public information, easy to copycat. Her gut said it was the Word Killer, but she struggled to reconcile the fact that he let Danielle live.

With practice, serial killers achieved better performances at subduing their victims, at timing their attacks, at tying up all the loose ends, and removing any evidence. They hesitated less when killing, enjoyed it more; never forfeited the kill, because it brought their ultimate release, the drug they craved with their entire being. A mistake of such magnitude didn't seem likely.

And yet, his latest victim was alive.

Tess followed Danielle's steps in the hallway toward the bathroom, then stopped short of stepping into a pool of almost-dried blood. The edges of the pool were smudged, matching Danielle's account of the attack. She'd been thrown to the floor and hit a small table with her head, getting the nasty cut on her neck. Then she lost consciousness, completely immobile, and bled on the granite tile floor.

The unsub must've thought she was dead, probably seeing the large amount of blood oozing from the back of her head, not knowing it was a flesh wound instead of a cracked skull.

Except, Danielle was not really dead.

The cold tiles had helped her regain consciousness, per her own account. Somehow, through a superhuman effort, she'd managed to sneak out of the house and scramble toward safety, while the Word Killer was busy with his enigmatic calligraphy.

Why did he stop midword? Tess asked herself, pacing the area slowly, careful not to disturb the scene too much, on the odd chance it would become an official crime scene at some point.

She approached the wall and studied the smudged letters closely. The letters A and O were the thickest, darkest ones, while the last letter he'd written, the N, was almost transparent.

He'd run out of blood.

When he went to get more from the victim, he saw she was gone and freaked out. He must've left the scene in a hurry, afraid the cops would show up any minute, unaware the woman would do anything to keep her ordeal a secret.

That meant he'd made more mistakes, ripe for the picking by Tess's keen senses.

She took photos of the scene, using a ten-dollar bill for scale reference. She took her time, studied every angle, traced every step the killer had taken inside the house. Once she left the premises, she couldn't have any unanswered questions.

She headed into the dining room, where Danielle said she'd been pinned face down against the table. On the carpet, next to the table leg, was a tiny white stain, starchy in appearance.

"Bingo," she whispered with a quick, satisfied laugh.

She turned on a small UV flashlight and shaded the area with her hand. The stain lit up under the UV, confirming it was biologic. Semen, by the looks of it. Satisfied, Tess rummaged through the kitchen drawers until she found a box cutter, removed a piece of the carpet and sealed it in an evidence bag.

She'd thoroughly collected everything, aware there was no crime scene unit to do its diligence at the scene, leaving her available for interviewing witnesses and chasing suspects. Now, ready to leave with an armful of evidence pouches, she found herself wondering how she was going to have it processed without a case number.

Chapter 6

Tess took the elevator down to the morgue, carrying the evidence bags neatly packed inside a large grocery bag. She carefully looked around at every step of the way, making a mental note of those who recognized and greeted her. Later, she might have to file a statement accounting for each step she took that day, if things went sour.

The morgue doors whooshed open, and she walked in, relieved to see no one was visiting with Doc Rizza at the time. The lights were off, except the doctor's desk lamp and a motion-sensor activated, fluorescent ceiling lamp that turned on with a faint click the moment she stepped in.

Doc Rizza sat on a four-legged stool in front of the sink, rinsing instruments. When he saw her approaching, he dropped them noisily and washed his hands.

"Agent Winnett, what an unexpected surprise," he greeted her, meeting her halfway with the gait of an old grizzly bear.

"Hello, Doc," she replied, smiling to hide her nervousness. "Is this a good time, or—"

"It's always a good time for you," he said, leading her to his desk.

The morgue showed signs of having been lived in, and not only by the deceased. There were two pillows and a blanket on a couch behind the desk. A nearly empty bottle of scotch and an empty glass were left on a small instrument table he'd pulled over to serve as a coffee table to keep the booze handy. On the cluttered desk, a photo of his late wife was placed so he could look straight at her charming face.

Since Mrs. Rizza had passed, Doc dreaded going home, or so

it was rumored. Now Tess could see why.

Seeing where her eyes were focusing, he scrambled to hide the bottle inside a drawer and mumbled an explanation. "I was working late last night, really late. Didn't make sense to, um, go home."

"No need to explain, Doc. This is your place; you make the rules."

"What can I do for you?" he asked, looking intently at the bag she was carrying.

She shifted her weight from one foot to the other, then paced in place a little. "The real question is, can you do it off the record?"

He frowned, a little confused. "As in…?"

"As in, I was never here, and you never looked at this evidence," she replied, gesturing at the bag. "Completely off the record."

Doc Rizza scratched the unruly tuft of hair at the center of his shiny scalp. "In my experience, things only go bad for serial killers when you ask me to do stuff off the record. Tell me what you need."

Tess pulled the Ziploc bag holding Danielle's blood-soaked robe. "I need DNA from this. My guess is it will match the DNA we have on file for the Word Killer, but I'd rather be sure. Somewhere, underneath all this blood, I'm sure we can find some semen. If not, we'll probably find it here instead," she added, handing him the small evidence bag with a 2-by-2–inch section of carpet.

Doc cleared the evidence processing table and pulled on fresh gloves. "Is that it?"

"Can I see the autopsy reports for the Word Killer's victims?"

He nodded and muttered, "Uh-huh," while carefully

extracting the robe from the bag. He examined it under UV light, then cut several small pieces from the cloth and put them in a vial. He removed several stained rug fibers and sealed them in another vial. He added chemicals from two bottles, carefully measured with a pipette, put the vials in a centrifuge, and pressed a green button. The centrifuge started whirring, increasing speed until it reached 3,000 rotations per minute.

"Did they call you in on the Word Killer?"

She shook her head.

"Ah, that's why the off-the-record bit; okay, I get it," he commented with a wicked grin. "Which one of his victims does this belong to?"

She shook her head again. "Sorry, Doc, it's better you don't know."

Two vertical ridges promptly appeared at the top of his nose while he stared at her with a scrutinizing glance. "Is this yours, my dear?" he whispered.

"Oh, God, no," Tess replied. "It's nothing like that." For a brief moment, she wondered if she looked like she'd nearly bled out recently. She hoped not.

"That's good to know," Doc Rizza replied with a quick sigh. "What else do you need? Ah, yes, autopsy reports, you said." He walked over to the large filing cabinet and rummaged through the files in the second drawer. He extracted three folders and joined Tess at the exam table, pulling up a chair and staring at the grocery bag. "What else have you got in there?"

"Um, we might not need to process the rest of the stuff. DNA is all I need, really," she added quickly, shifting her eyes sideways. "What's your analysis of his MO?"

"The attacks were brutal and sudden; the sexual assaults violent and prolonged. There's little evidence of defensive wounds because the victims were quickly overpowered. The carvings were done antemortem, and in all three cases, the cause of death was blunt force trauma."

"Spells out a lot of anger, doesn't it?" Tess asked.

"Indeed, it does; but you're the profiler, not me. I'm just the coroner. You speculate and theorize, while I state only scientifically proven facts."

"What's your opinion on the carvings?" she asked, ignoring his previous statement. She still wanted him to ruminate with her, to brainstorm ideas about the killer's motivations, his true intentions.

Doc Rizza steepled his hands in front of him and whistled as if to express the question was a challenging one. "This son of a bitch has a message to communicate to us, to the world. He carves these symbols on his victims' bodies; he writes in blood on their walls. We haven't a clue what the messages mean, while he gets to euphorically believe he's the smartest at this game."

"If we want to catch him, we need to understand his messages," Tess replied, then grabbed a sheet of paper from the printer and the pen from Doc Rizza's chest pocket. "May I?" she asked after the fact with a quick smile. "Let's write it down. What did the bastard carve?"

"On Mandy Alvarado's body," Doc read from the first file, "he carved 2M."

Tess wrote it on the paper. "Then?"

"Earlene, the pilot, had 5W cut on her back."

"Always in the same place?"

"Always above the left buttock," Doc confirmed. "Then, he wrote 1M on Christi Connor's back."

Tess wrote 1M on the paper, then, after the pen hesitated

midair for a long moment, she wrote 3D below the other three entries without putting in Danielle's name.

Doc sprung to his feet. "Is there another victim?" he asked, not taking his eyes from the paper.

"Sorry, but I can't say. All I can tell you is that no one died without making it to your autopsy table," she offered, instantly regretting even sharing that much information. Doc wasn't stupid; he would find two strands of DNA in the samples provided. What if Danielle was in some DNA registry? Millions of people had voluntarily sent their DNA to ancestry services, not knowing that those services had built databases they readily sold to anyone who wanted to have the information. As such, even if Danielle didn't have a record, her DNA, or one of her close family members' DNA, could be in the system. Someone like Doc Rizza wouldn't need more to find out everything she wasn't sharing.

She needed to be more careful and share nothing of what she knew.

"What do you see in these symbols, Doc?" she asked, but received no reply; only a quick, frustrated glance. She wrung her hands for a while, wondering if it could be that simple. "I see, M, W, and D, and I'm thinking months, weeks, and days."

"Until when?"

"That, we don't know yet," she said, feeling frustration overcome her brief sense of accomplishment. "Let's assume I'm right and map the timeline, then we'll see if anything matches. The first victim, Mandy, when did she die?"

"Um, on January third, precisely two months ago yesterday."

"That means, if I'm right and the carvings on her back mean two months, then something should've happened yesterday, but what? Can you please check?"

If the carvings were about time, they didn't refer to other girls being attacked. Even if Danielle had been assaulted exactly two months after Mandy, that seemed to be a coincidence, because Earlene was attacked after Mandy, three and a half weeks later. If the carvings were really about time, they had to represent something else, something she didn't know of. Something to do with Mandy.

He pulled over his laptop and opened the system, then accessed the case file. "No mention of any event or case log entry with yesterday's date."

"Damn, I thought I knew what the carvings were about," Tess mumbled. "How about the second victim, the pilot?"

"Earlene was killed on January twenty-eighth," Doc replied. "If 5W means five weeks, that would be, um, today. For whatever that means."

"Today? Are you sure?"

"Positive," he replied, gesturing at the calendar open on his laptop.

"And the third one?"

"Christi Connor was killed on February twenty-fourth, and one month from that would make it March twenty-fourth. Whatever this is, we won't know for a while."

"If I'm right and these are time references, Doc. Because I might be wrong."

"I can't remember a time when you were wrong," he replied with a kind smile. "How about the mystery entry, 3D? What date is that running from?"

She hesitated for a long moment. "Yesterday."

"So, the day after tomorrow, I guess?"

"Yeah," she replied. "We'll know soon enough." She walked over to the back wall, then returned to the table, restless, frustrated about her own powerlessness. Every minute she wasted not understanding what the unsub's message meant, the bastard walked free, stalking his next victim, getting ready to kill again.

She'd seen his sort, studied it at large, and put his kind behind bars or into the ground, every damn time. It was a matter of understanding how the unsub thought, what he felt, and anticipating what his next move was going to be.

He must've been a male in his thirties, white—based on the race of his victims—and a sadistic lust killer. He'd evolved into the state he was now, and his rage was fueled by something in his past, an event that profilers called a trigger. His victims didn't share a common physiognomy. Mandy was a brunette with green eyes, Earlene had hazel eyes and dark brown hair, and Christi was a freckled redhead with brown eyes. As for Danielle, she had auburn-blonde hair and blue eyes. Nothing in common.

Tess's colleague, SA Patto, had done his diligence regarding the victims' backgrounds, and the three girls couldn't've been further apart. They'd never gone to the same schools, shops, restaurants, or hair salons. Tess reviewed the first victim's background in detail; it was common to find a serial killer who started killing with a victim he met by accident, in his close circle, whether social or geographical. But there was nothing of the sort she could find. The accountant, single mom had minimal interactions with anyone outside her work and the functions of her daughter's rearing.

Based on the information contained in the detailed backgrounds, the three victims had never crossed paths, nor had they shared any commonality.

That left Tess with the extra bit of information she'd

gathered from Danielle.

"Doc, is there a reference anywhere on those case files to the name Delilah?"

"Ah, I see you heard the recording," Doc reacted, puzzling Tess. "What an amazing thing, to be able to do that, right?"

"What are you talking about?"

"You don't know about the recording?" He saw the baffled look on Tess's face continuing to linger, and he clarified in a softer, less excited voice. "They retrieved a recording of Christi Conner's assault."

"What recording?"

"Christi had one of those Alexa digital virtual assistants. She must've said something during the attack that made the device start recording everything. That's how we learned that the unsub repeatedly called Christi by the name Delilah during the assault. I also heard with my own ears how brutal it was; it's nearly unbearable to listen to."

Tess made an impatient gesture with her hand, and Doc started the playback on his computer with a loud sigh.

Over the next few minutes, cringing and wishing she could tear the speakers to pieces, Tess listened to the sounds of Christi Connor screaming and pleading while being raped and then killed. The unsub laughed like a madman, made threats, spilled his rage, and called the victim Delilah. He'd said, "How do you like it now, Delilah? How's that avarice working for you now? You'll never forget me, I swear, Delilah."

The end of the recording brought silence, heavy and troublesome, interrupted only by the whirring of the centrifuge. Tess stood, went around the exam table and hit the red button on the machine.

"No need to run DNA now, Doc. I've just confirmed what I

needed to confirm."

She waited for the machine to stop spinning, and the lid popped open. She extracted the two vials and slid them into her pocket, under Doc Rizza's stunned eyes.

"There's a survivor," Rizza whispered, slack-jawed. "You found a survivor, didn't you?"

"Shhh," she urged him with a finger pressed against her lips.

"I've already promised," he replied, seeming a little offended with her lack of confidence.

"What I wouldn't give to know what Delilah stands for. What does the name represent? Is she a woman from the unsub's past? She's most likely someone who did him wrong in a meaningful way."

"In the Hebrew Bible, Delilah was a betrayer. The great Samson loved her, but she revealed the source of his power to the Philistines and cut his hair. Consequently, Samson's vigor was lost, and he was captured, I believe. Captured or killed by the Philistines."

"Do you think the unsub has religious motives?" Tess asked.

"I thought of it, because of the words he leaves written on the wall. Those resemble, to some extent, the seven deadly sins. Avarice is one, and we saw that in Christi's case. Lust is another deadly sin, and so is greed. As a deadly sin, greed is equated with avarice."

"Not only as a deadly sin, but I believe the thesaurus also equates the two notions," she replied thoughtfully. "But the unsub used different variants the concept, avarice and greed. What's the difference?"

"Avarice is more of a financial nature, while greed could be any form of overconsumption, including food or drink," Doc replied.

"I didn't know you were a word wiz, Doc."

"I do crosswords a lot lately. Nothing else to do with myself at night since…" His voice trailed off, and his shoulders dropped. "Anyway, in the unlikely circumstance there was a survivor that you might or might not know about, was there a word on that hypothetical person's wall?"

Tess smiled at the convoluted way he asked the question. He'd earned her trust on many occasions; against her initial commitment, she decided she was going to show that. "Arrogance."

"Ah, another deadly sin," Doc replied. "How interesting."

"I can't figure out how they connect. These women had done nothing in their lives to justify those words. Nothing that I could find."

"Keep looking, Tess. You'll find him, I know you will."

He stood with a groan and vigorously rubbed his back as he straightened with difficulty. He pointed at the bag of evidence. "What should I do with these?"

"I can't ask you to store them without a case number," she replied, reluctantly grabbing the bag.

"Sure you can, if this is what you need me to do," he replied. "I'll store them with today's date instead of a case number, and we'll see where that goes. If it goes nowhere, in one year from today, I'll cremate the entire box. No record of it anywhere, no questions asked. By then, I trust the Word Killer will be history."

She extracted the two vials from her pocket and handed them over. "Thanks, Doc. I've got to run."

"Where to?" he asked, walking her to the door.

"It's time to talk to the men in those women's lives," she replied. "Even if it's not officially my case. Maybe the men were the targets."

"What made you think of that? The men weren't harmed."

"The story of Samson, and how he was defeated by a woman's betrayal. The unsub punishes the Delilah in his life over and over again, but he somehow might be targeting the Philistines. Like any villain in a good story, I'm sure they were guilty of more than one deadly sin."

Chapter 7

It was still early, and there was a good chance she'd find Mandy Alvarado's boyfriend, Allan Brehm, at his posh office downtown. While she drove there, Donovan read her everything he had about Brehm. He was fifty-two years old, a bit of an age difference from Mandy, who was only twenty-seven. He was a successful real estate developer, who'd built hotels and resorts in Miami Beach and Palm Beach over the past thirty years. Rumors had it he was ruthless, forcing older property owners out of their homes if he wanted to cheaply acquire the properties.

Donovan's research put Brehm's net assets somewhere over the two-billion-dollar mark.

In short, he was a greedy son of a bitch.

Huh, Tess thought. Maybe it's a coincidence, just like the fact that none of the Word Killer's victims had been married. No, they were all dating and had wealthy boyfriends. She wondered if that was relevant; probably it was, a critical piece of the victimology puzzle she needed to keep in mind.

She entered the high-rise property bearing the Brehm Realty Investments logo in gold lettering and headed straight for the reception desk. There, she presented her ID and frowned when she saw the receptionist's reaction.

"I need to see Mr. Brehm immediately," Tess said. "This is important."

Flustered, the receptionist let her mouth gape for a fraction of a second, then picked up the phone. Dialing, she mumbled, "Oh, I thought you knew."

Tess touched the phone cradle with a finger, ending the

call the receptionist was making before it connected. "Knew what?"

"Mr. Brehm died last night," she said, keeping her voice a low whisper, and looking left and right as if she'd been instructed to keep the tycoon's death a secret.

"How did he die?"

"Severe allergic reaction," the receptionist said. "His steak was tainted with shellfish."

In other words, he'd been poisoned.

"Who had access to his property?"

"Oh, he didn't eat at home last night," she whispered, bringing her head closer to Tess.

"Where did he eat?"

"At his favorite restaurant, the Aji Hibachi."

Tess scoffed. "Let me get this straight. He was allergic to shellfish, yet he chose to have steak at a Japanese restaurant?"

"He'd been eating there for years, and there was never an issue."

"What about an EpiPen? Didn't he carry one of those?"

The girl shrugged. "Sorry, I don't know anything about that. His executive assistant might know more."

But Tess was already rushing out of the building. Brehm's death meant two things. One, she'd been right about the carvings; they were dates, death dates for the boyfriends if she could venture to draw a conclusion based on a single data point. But to consider it a coincidence would've been too much. Two, the five-week warning that had been carved on Earlene Burnett's body expired today, and that meant her boyfriend, none other than the famous Elias Mosley, was next to die.

Nowhere in the messages the Word Killer had left behind was it stated the deadlines ran out at night. Elias Mosley could be dead already.

She ran all the way to her SUV and was about to call Donovan when a call from Pearson came through.

"Sir," she greeted the caller, rolling her eyes in frustration. She didn't have any time to spare.

"Where are we with BCI Insurance?"

"Who?" she blurted before she realized what she was saying.

"Jeez, Winnett, you're unbelievable. Give me one good reason why I shouldn't fire you right now, over the phone. Please tell me you've been looking into the fraud case I assigned to you."

"Y—yes, I have."

"Really? Have you talked to anyone at BCI yet?"

Lying to Pearson was only going to make matters worse. "No, sir, I haven't," she reluctantly admitted.

"Then, what the hell have you been doing all day?"

She let a long moment pass, already knowing how Pearson would react to what she had to say.

"I've been looking into the Word murders. I have a theory—"

"Patto has a theory I'd want to hear, Winnett, not you," he snapped. "You know why? Because Patto is the agent assigned to the Word murders, not you."

"But, sir—"

"Do you have a theory about BCI's fraudulent health plans? That's what I want to hear from you, and nothing else."

She munched on her lip, thinking how best to get her boss to cooperate.

"Elias Mosley will die tonight. If he's not already dead."

"How do you know?"

"It's a long story, but—"

"Tell me."

"The victim's skin carvings represent time, time elapsed

between the day the girls die and the day their boyfriends die. Allan Brehm died last night."

"I'm not following," Pearson replied, as usual, frustrated when he was missing information.

"The M in the carvings stands for months, the W for weeks, the D for days."

"What D?" he asked. "There's no carved D on any of the bodies."

"Uh, no specific D, just theoretically, if he were to kill a victim and carve a D on her back, that would stand for days," she quickly unloaded a statement that had to be the lamest lie told by an agent in the entire history of the FBI. Even a rookie could've caught it; Pearson, for some reason, decided to let it slide with a minute of silence and a request that threw her off.

"Talk to Patto about this. Work with him."

She knew she should've replied, "Yes, sir," but couldn't.

"I work better alone, sir," she replied instead; she could sense the air vibrating with the electricity of Pearson's irritation. "I can't manage his bruised ego and hunt for a serial killer at the same time. Mosley could already be dead by now."

She heard him mumbling an oath under his breath.

"All right, you have twenty-four hours," he replied in a cold, menacing tone. "I'll manage Patto's rightfully bruised ego, because I just love cleaning up your messes, Winnett. It's what I live for."

He ended the call without warning, the modern equivalent of a slammed phone receiver.

She breathed, wondering if she would have a job after the case was over. She hoped so; that was everything she had. She was beginning to sense she was approaching the end of the line with Pearson at an accelerated rate.

After she'd caught the Word Killer, she'd play things by the book for a year, she promised herself. Do whatever Pearson wanted, however Pearson wanted it, and get back into his good graces.

She started driving toward the freeway while calling Donovan.

"Hey, D," she said the moment the analyst took the call. "I need the location of Elias Mosley and a way to get to him, pronto."

"The actor?" Donovan reacted. "He's, like, one of the top paid actors of last year. How exactly would you like me to do that? He could be anywhere; shooting an action scene in Hollywood, flying on his personal jet, or cruising the Atlantic in that yacht of his."

"Track his phone, his credit card, whatever it takes. Get Patto to show up there, pronto. We need to get to Mosley before the Word Killer does."

Chapter 8

She expected many things, but not the magnetism of Elias Mosley's real-life persona. He was charismatic; if the word had a superlative, it would spell out Mosley's name. She could easily understand how a young woman like Earlene could fall head over heels for him, despite the fact they were worlds apart. He was an actor, while she'd served as one of the youngest female first officers on a Boeing 737 aircraft. She didn't fly for one of the commercial airlines; for a reason that would probably remain unexplained now that she was gone, instead she chose to pilot for one of the major freight couriers.

Tess waited in a stunning living room in the actor's Palm Beach residence, feeling a little intimidated, an unfamiliar state of mind for the rather calloused FBI agent. She paced slowly along the walls, taking in the display of personal photographs, framed and hung tastefully in clusters by topic. There was Mosley, accepting his Oscar last year, then radiating at the after-party, Earlene at his side. Then, the two of them on a vacation around the world, photographed against a backdrop of recognizable landmarks, such as the Pyramids, the Great Wall of China, the Eiffel Tower, and Mount Olympus.

"She always flew, but I drove," she heard Mosley's unmistakable voice behind her. She turned to face him. "Whenever we traveled together," he clarified, "she'd be the one behind the throttle. I loved to watch her fly."

"I'm very sorry for your loss, Mr. Mosley," she said, showing her badge.

He gestured toward a bunch of large, white leather armchairs and she took a seat, sinking comfortably into the soft cushions.

"Tell me, Agent Winnett, what can I do for you?"

To her disbelief, the famous Elias Mosley, who'd been dubbed, "Sexiest Man Alive" only two years ago, was looking her over. His eyes lingered on certain parts of her body, then spent a good deal of time focused on her cleavage. When he finally looked straight at her, his lips were parted in a sexy, inviting smile.

Lust.

She remembered the word written on Earlene's wall. It was lust. And it was his sin, not hers. Just like greed was Brehm's sin.

She grinned. "You just answered one big question already, but I have more."

"Shoot," he replied, crossing his legs and widening his sexy smile just a little bit, as if he were on a TV show, answering questions from fans.

"How did you two meet?"

"At LAX," he replied. "The Los Angeles airport, that is. We both flew in at the same time. Me in my measly Phenom 300, and she in her imposing 737, towering over me on the tarmac. I was instantly in awe of her."

"Aren't you married, Mr. Mosley?"

"Ah, you're judging?"

"Not in the least. But someone killed your girlfriend, and it's not unusual to question the relationships in a victim's life."

"She was killed by a serial killer, wasn't she? My wife is not a serial killer, I promise you that."

Tess groaned, but couldn't hide a smile. The man's charm was infectious. "So, yes, you're married."

"Uh-huh, I am."

"Where does your wife live?"

"In our home in Santa Monica."

"And you?"

"I followed Earlene here. Miami was her home, and I fell in love with everything Earlene, including Miami."

"Please walk me through your last few days with Earlene. Where you went, any new people you met, places you visited. I'm looking for any possible place where the killer could've met her, you, or both."

"As you know, she died on January twenty-eighth," he said, his smile now gone, and his voice tinged with sadness. "Up until two days prior to that, she had a long-haul flight to Buenos Aires and back. She was gone for four days. Then, on the twenty-seventh, we went out boating, only the two of us. We took the small boat, to be by ourselves."

"Where did you go?"

"Nowhere in particular. Just out there, toward the Bahamas, but we didn't get close to its shores. We just enjoyed being together, the two of us and the sea, not seeing anyone, not talking to anyone. It was beautiful. If I'd only known it was our last time on the water together…" His voice trailed off, and his shoulders dropped as he leaned into his elbows, hiding his face in his hands.

"How about the next day? Do you recall anything?"

"Every minute," he replied. "We slept in late and ate inside. I got sunburned the day before, while on our boat. We splashed in the pool and didn't go out, not until dinner."

"Where was that?" Tess asked with a frown, realizing that Agent Patto's case notes didn't include that information.

"We went to the Solstice. My assistant managed to get us a last-minute reservation."

Of course, he did. Restaurants would pay to have a star of Mosley's magnitude dine at one of their tables.

"How is that place? I've heard many things, but never went."

"It's amazing. Go, if you have the opportunity. It's pricey but well worth it. Every type of menu is an experience. You can choose molecular gastronomy, American, exotic, Asian fusion, and you won't regret a single bite."

Tess smiled. "Maybe, one day, who knows."

"I'd be happy to—"

Tess stopped his advances with an abrupt hand gesture. Was he devastated after the loss of his girlfriend? Or was he already back in the dating game only five weeks after her demise?

"Listen to me, Mr. Mosley, and listen carefully. The killer might be out to get you next."

"What?"

Blood drained from his face. He stood abruptly and shoved his hands in his pockets, then went to the windows and looked outside, as if the killer would attack his home from the beach.

"Do you have your own security?"

"Yes, I do. I have two—"

"Call them, and make sure they're with you at all times, even if you go to the bathroom. Tonight, when you sleep, they'll be in the room with you. Is that clear?"

He wasn't smiling anymore, and any trace of sexy playfulness had disappeared from his face.

"Yeah, it's clear."

"We'll have an agent with you shortly, and you'll be safe if you take minimum precautions until we get this man."

She stated that firmly and without any hesitation, wondering when exactly she would get her hands on the Word Killer.

"Don't accept food or beverages from strangers; don't go out; don't accept deliveries, gifts, or anything."

"Yeah, yeah, I got it. Maybe I should go back to California."

"We can't protect you in California, Mr. Mosley. Those of us who know and understand the Word Killer are here in Florida."

"Understood."

She stood, getting ready to leave. Would he be safe if the killer missed the deadline? Or would the bastard come after him again and again, until he was dead, paying for his lust?

"Um, Agent Winnett, how exactly will he try to kill me?"

"I have no idea," she replied candidly. "Anything is possible, from poison to sniper fire, but we won't let anything happen to you, I'm sure of it."

That last part was where her candor vanished. She had no idea how to protect Mosley, and she didn't believe he'd be safe in protective custody. Someone with his disruptive potential as a celebrity was safest among the people who didn't fall over themselves whenever he smiled.

She wasted a few more minutes until Agent Patto finally showed up. Patto glared at her without a word as he passed her on the doorstep, then went inside the mansion with an excited grin on his lips.

Chapter 9

They had to pull Winston Whitfield out of a board meeting, and he was furious. His assistant apologized profusely, yet he scolded her, nevertheless, keeping his tone down, yet pouring enough acid in his voice to leave permanent marks.

He was the youngest of the victim's boyfriends, at only thirty-six years old, the CEO of the family business, a three-generation industrial equipment conglomerate worth a couple of billion. Tess didn't give him the benefit of the doubt; she examined the approaching man for signs of the avarice the Word Killer held against him, knowing for sure they were there to be found.

Probably. So far, she only saw immense, exasperating arrogance. Christi Conner seemed sweet, gentle, and charming, at least based on the videos of the socialite Tess had seen. What could Christi have seen in this tyrant? Whitfield seemed dark and dangerous, maybe in a Fifty Shades of Grey kind of way. Maybe. So far, Tess only saw his all-consuming anger on display; nothing else.

"Who are you again?" he asked before he reached her, the distance between them a justification for his elevated tone. "How dare you interrupt my board meeting?"

Unimpressed, Tess flashed her badge. "Unless you want to do this at headquarters, I suggest you answer a few questions."

As expected, that statement poured some ice water over his flaming ego.

"What do you need?"

"A step-by-step account of your last few days with Christi. Places you went, people you met, that kind of thing."

This aspect of the interview was missing from Agent Patto's notes, although he'd interviewed Whitfield after Christi's death. However, his notes stopped abruptly after the question regarding the man's whereabouts at the time of the murder. Judging by his demeanor, that must've been the moment he lawyered up, and Patto must've deemed the issue not worth pursuing any further.

"She died six days ago," he said. "The day before that was a Monday, and we both worked 'til late at night. She was covering a fashion show at the Penthouse at Riverside Wharf, and I was on a conference call with Tokyo. We met late at night at the house."

"Hers? Or yours?"

"Mine," he replied with a quick nose crinkle, as if to express his low opinion of the girl's house. "We only spent time at my place."

"Then?"

"The day she died, we celebrated. Her show coverage was a success; her videos were downloaded in the millions; and my deal with Tokyo was signed. That afternoon, we rode horses on the beach at Sunny Isles, then later we went out for a long dinner."

"Where?"

"At that new fancy restaurant downtown, Solstice. We had—" He stopped midphrase, seemingly stunned. "Agent Winnett!"

Tess had turned away, rushing toward the elevators. Impatiently pressing the down button, she grinned. There was one point of commonality in the victims' backgrounds after all, and that meant she had a lead.

Chapter 10

Tess stormed out of the building, the call with Donovan already active. She had a lead, the restaurant where two of the victims had dined the last night of their lives. She wanted to call Danielle and confirm the pattern, but she made the call to Donovan a priority, to give him more time to zero in on the unsub.

"State your business," he said instead of a greeting. "Glad you came clean with the boss, by the way," he added before she could voice her request. "It felt as if I was about to be fired, and that's not a good feeling."

"I still feel like I'm about to get fired," she reacted. "But maybe we can avoid that."

"What do you need?"

"Two of the vics had dinner at Solstice the night they died. Let's make sure the third one did too," she said.

"Why wasn't this information in the victimology background?"

"I'm not sure. At first glance, I'd say because the boyfriends paid for the dinner, and the initial background only included the victims' financials. Hence, it never showed up."

"Huh," he said, too professional to make a comment about what appeared to be sloppy work by another analyst. "Maybe they're still working on it."

"Mandy Alvarado's boyfriend, Allan Brehm, would've paid for their meals on January third. That is if I'm right."

She stopped talking, while Donovan typed quickly, whistling his interpretation of a familiar song.

Walking swiftly, she arrived at her SUV and climbed behind

the wheel, then switched the call over to the Ford's media center.

"Bingo," Donovan announced. "They were there, the credit card transaction time stamp is 7:48 p.m. I know what to do next. Backgrounds for everyone there, including parking valets and back room temps."

"Yup, you got it." She drove off toward the freeway, heading toward downtown Miami. She wanted to be at the restaurant's door when Donovan gave her the name she was waiting for.

"We have a bit of a problem," he announced. "There are seventy-eight employees at the Solstice. I knew the place was huge, but I didn't expect this number."

"Let's narrow it down," Tess replied. "First, exclude all female workers."

"Already done. Thirty-seven men left."

"Exclude anyone who's not Caucasian."

"That leaves us with twenty-one people."

"Get rid of those who are under twenty-five and over forty."

"Aren't you taking a risk here? What if your profile is wrong, even just a little bit?"

Donovan didn't know about Danielle, and he wasn't going to find out. Tess trusted Danielle's estimation of the man's age.

"I'll take my chances this time."

"Okay, but it didn't do much. We're down to nineteen men."

"Now, let's bring the big guns. Cross-reference with the name Delilah. Could've been his mother, sister, wife, or daughter. I'm betting on mother."

He typed for a while in a foreboding silence. "Nope, it doesn't show up."

Damn… she'd been sure about that piece of the profile.

"Okay," she sighed, "let's go old school. Anyone with a

criminal record for sexual assault? Or any rap sheet, for that matter."

"No such luck," Donovan replied. "Apparently, Solstice screens their employees really well."

"Then we're down to one more thing we haven't tried."

"What?"

"Let's find out which of these employees were on duty when the victims were there to dine: January third, January twenty-eighth, February twenty-fourth, and—"

"And?" Donovan asked. "I thought that's all we had, three victims."

She almost swore out loud. "Yeah, you're right. Let's find out who was there and saw those girls at Solstice."

"If you don't want me to call the restaurant, it will take a while to find out. I'll have to access the restaurant's attendance system and get the info from there."

Tess checked the time and frowned. It was almost six, and the Word Killer would soon go after Mosley unless he found another woman whose boyfriend reminded him of who knows what bastard in his life, and he tortured and killed her while calling her Delilah. She couldn't risk that. She couldn't risk another life.

"You know what? I have a better idea. How would you like to see some action? You always wanted to be a field agent, right?"

A moment of silence ensued, and Tess visualized him taking a gulp of fruit water from his enormous travel mug with its double-layered, transparent exterior.

"What did you have in mind?"

"Mosley invited me to Solstice for dinner. I could say yes and go there with him, but I'd rather go with you instead. How soon can you get dressed to the nines and get us a limo?"

"Whoa… You want to put yourself as bait? And use me as bait too? I don't really know how I feel about this."

"Don't worry," Tess laughed. "The male part of the duo always lives. At least for a while. You'll be safe."

"Can you think of doing this another way?"

"The only other way is to use Mosley. I could pose as his new girlfriend. Pearson would have my ass and my badge in a breakfast sandwich the moment he heard I put a civilian in harm's way. So, no, not really. Can't think of another way."

"I need to get Pearson's approval before we proceed," Donovan said.

"Um, listen, this time, let's go for apologizing later instead of asking first. We don't have time to waste. The killer might've already met his new target."

"He never stalks the victims? Never does homework?"

"Not that I've seen in the files. He seems impulsive, relying on violence and the surprise of a flash attack. My guess is he follows his target as she leaves the restaurant, then enters her house and kills her."

"How does he know the vics live alone?"

That was an excellent question.

"Maybe he doesn't, or maybe he's willing to take the chance and kill however many people stand in his way to rape and kill Delilah all over again."

"I thought of that, you know," he said. "I thought he might've killed his Delilah first. But I couldn't find any rape-murder victim named Delilah in the past forty years, and I looked nationwide. It's not a common name."

"Maybe he hasn't killed her, his Delilah. Maybe he keeps killing substitutes ever since she betrayed him. A lot of maybes, D, but one thing is for sure. Any moment now, the Word Killer will strike again."

A moment of silence filled the air, but it was a brief one.

"Okay. I'll do it," Donovan replied, excitement bubbling in his voice once he'd agreed with it.

"Good. Let's think of a sin for you. How would you like greed, like Allan Brehm? The unsub went for that big time."

"I'm not sure what that entails," he replied.

"Let me worry about that. You get the tux and the limo ready and meet me in downtown Miami in forty-five minutes. You have a date."

She ended the call and soon after that she exited the freeway, heading downtown. She pulled in at a ritzy hair salon, where she had to wield her badge like a weapon to get a stylist to do her hair and makeup without an appointment.

Almost thirty minutes later, she sat under a hairdryer, while on the phone with Danielle and Cat. They had the phone on speaker mode so they could both converse with Tess.

Danielle too had eaten dinner at Solstice, and the night of her attack was the first time she or Stephen had dined there. No one had drawn her attention, and she couldn't recall if any of the employees or the people she met there were her attacker. Her memory was still a blur.

Danielle told Tess she had called her fiancé and told him she was traveling to see her sick grandmother, and he could carry on with his father's campaign travels instead of rushing back home. As such, she hoped she'd be back on her feet by the time he returned, the house cleaned of bloodstains, and her vitality regained. Although, she cried, the carvings on her back would leave a permanent scar she'd have a difficult time explaining.

Tess urged them both to be careful and not take any risks. Cat promised her they would, the bar would stay closed for the evening. Then Cat had taken the phone from Danielle and went downstairs so he could ask her in private, "What's your plan, kiddo?"

"I'm going after him tonight, Cat. By ten or eleven, I hope the bastard will be gone. To jail, that is," she corrected herself, although she didn't anticipate the unsub would allow himself to be taken alive. Power-assertive sadists almost never do.

"And how do you plan on doing that?"

"I'll just have dinner, looking pretty and showing off a rich man. I hope that will get him to come after me."

He went silent for a while. "I know this is what you do for a living, but please take care. How many people are watching your back?"

"I promise I'll be fine," she replied, then ended that call and connected to the next one.

Before going shopping for an evening dress and some heels, she wanted to know if SA Patto was still doing his job, guarding Elias Mosley.

Turned out, he was. He barely spoke two words with her, but she didn't need more.

She sent a text to Donovan giving him the address of where to meet her, conveniently neglecting to mention it was a beauty salon.

Chapter 11

Donovan looked as if he hated the moment that he'd agreed to take part in Tess's plans. He sat in a salon chair, surrounded by stylists, feeling totally out of place. It was a women's salon, and all the other patrons gave him long stares. But Tess's persuasion skills, paired with another flash of her badge, a reference to "a matter of life and death," and a couple of well-targeted threats had eventually secured the full cooperation of the staff at Love My 'Do.

Tess held up her phone with a recent photo of the famous Curtis Finch displayed, so the stylist could know what she was aiming for. She'd chosen Finch carefully, thinking of who best to lure the unsub in, someone who's reputation for insatiable greed preceded him, but also someone around Donovan's age. The thirty-year-old founder of one of the largest social media networks in the world was absolutely perfect.

"And what did you say this was called?" Donovan asked, turning a couple of shades redder in the face.

Two of the stylists giggled.

"A slick back and quiff," the one working on him replied.

He shot Tess a long, burning glare via the mirror. "You're so going to owe me, for, like, ever," he mumbled.

"As soon as we're done, we'll get you back in here or wherever else you want to go and change it back to the way it was. Okay?"

She waited for an answer from him, but none came, only another glare.

"It's hair, for crying out loud. Whatever it is, it will grow back. In your case, they're not even cutting much; just styling it over your head like that… like Justin Bieber, really."

"Winnett!" he snapped, looking more miserable than ever.

She decided to lay off him.

"Remember why we're here doing this, all right? Do you think I like wearing what I'm wearing?"

Tess had gone to an upscale boutique a few shops away from the hair salon. She'd bought a backless lace dress in navy blue, hemmed well above the knee, and had paired it with 4-inch heeled sandals with thin straps that cut into her toes and made her curse under her breath at every step. She had to give up her service weapon and had tucked the backup Sig in a thigh holster she'd never worn so high.

However uncomfortable, she could pull it off for a couple of hours. If only she could remember she was Delilah, a traitress, a woman who'd sided with the enemy to hurt the man who loved her.

Another stylist took care of her makeup, surprised when asked to make Tess look on the obvious side of cheap, but she obliged. She delivered what Tess happily admitted was a classy kind of trashy look in under ten minutes. By the time she was ready, so was Donovan.

In the back of the limo, she had exactly seven minutes to get him prepped and ready with his backstory before they reached the restaurant.

"You're a social media mega-tech gazillionaire, the Curtis Finch," she said, "as you might already know from your matching hairstyle."

"You had to choose that piece of—"

"He's an excellent choice if we want to bait the Word Killer. Finch is famously greedy; Forbes puts his fortune at seventy billion dollars, while half his employees sleep in their cars because he won't pay them enough to make rent in Silicon Valley. He's also a notorious ass, so please behave as such. Here," she reached into the pants abandoned on the limo seat in front of her and searched the pocket. She pulled out a wad of crispy cash folded in half and clipped in place, all hundred-dollar bills, twenty-two in all. "I drained my bank account, and I was lucky to find a banker who was willing to give me new bills. Flash that cash, but please don't spend it all. I need to pay my mortgage this month."

He took it and put it in his jacket pocket. "What else?"

"Wear these shades at all times," she said, offering him a pair she'd bought, chosen to resemble one of Finch's favorite sunglasses. "Your eyes are different than his; warmer, kinder."

"Uh-huh," he said, putting them on.

"Remember the part you're playing. You've seen Finch many times on TV. Be just as obnoxious, loud, and blatantly arrogant, and you'll do fine. I had someone make a call as if from a newspaper, asking when Finch was coming for dinner, so everyone in there is already primed and ready."

"Great," he muttered, visibly tense and a little pale.

Once he climbed out of the limo, his entire attitude changed. He seamlessly entered the part, playing Finch to perfection. Tess didn't have to fake the beaming smile she threw him when he held out his hand for her.

They were greeted by a host and hostess duo, fussing over them as expected. The hostess hugged Donovan with her eyes and would've readily fainted if he'd shown her the slightest sign of attention.

Donovan continued playing his part well, including slipping the host a one-hundred dollar bill and asking, "Put us somewhere peaceful, willya? I'm so damn tired of people yapping around me."

The host nodded and took them to a table with a "Reserved" card on it. The restaurant was full, almost all the tables occupied. There wasn't much of a seating choice, but the host still asked if the table was good enough. As he seated them, he gave Tess a long, appreciative look that brought a smile to her lips. That was how Delilah would most likely react; she'd thrive on male attention.

She was getting plenty of that; every passing waiter and customer plunging their eyes in her deep cleavage, then wrapping their lustful glances around her body where the dress ran backless, lower than she cared for.

If I ever want to start dating again, this is where I'll come, and this is what I'll wear, Tess found herself thinking with amusement while flipping through the luxurious pages of the menu.

She tried not to stare at every staff member who walked through the dining room. Any of them could've been the unsub, and he wasn't going to wear a sign stating that fact. If she stared too much, she risked spooking him. She focused on her partner instead and touched his hand with her fingers.

He flinched.

"Winnett, what the hell," he reacted.

"Just go with it, Curtis," she invited with an inviting smile, running her fingers up and down Donovan's hand, then in seductive little circles.

Donovan repressed a grin and raised his hand, then snapped his fingers. A waiter appeared by his side in under three seconds.

He pulled out the stack of money and took his time extracting a hundred-dollar bill.

"You see that couple over there? The fat redhead and the lame, bald guy? Move them somewhere else, willya? That woman's voice is driving me crazy. I can't eat like this."

"Yes, sir," the waiter bowed and then disappeared. Moments later, someone dressed in a black jacket, probably the manager, approached the couple and asked them to move. From what Tess could overhear, the manager had to foot their bill in exchange for their cooperation.

Donovan ordered for Tess, the typical behavior of a power freak, and she complied with a radiant smile. A line of waiters took turns filling their glasses with vintage champagne and delivering an impressive choice of appetizers. Everything was delicious.

When they brought his steak au poivre with thin, hand-cut fries, Donovan immediately sliced through it and pushed it back toward the waiter.

"Does this look like medium to you? This cow's about to start screaming. Are you trying to make me sick or something?"

"My apologies, sir. I'll take it right back—"

"And bring me reheated steak? Are you kidding me? Is this how you treat people here, in this joint? What are you, a fast food chain?"

The manager appeared out of thin air. "We'll take everything away, and redo both your orders, from scratch. In the meantime, please accept another selection of appetizers, on me."

Donovan stared at the man for a long moment. "Yeah... whatever."

The waitstaff cleaned the table and started over, bringing appetizers, and later, a steak grilled to perfection for Donovan and glazed salmon for Tess. This time, he accepted it with a grunt.

They ate, and nothing happened. They romanced as if they were on a first date; they laughed, sometimes loudly like people do when they don't care about anything in the world.

And nothing happened.

After having spent a little over two hours in the place, they left, hand in hand, giggling and leaning into each other, and then climbed into the limo that waited at the curb.

After it set in motion, they let their smiles wane.

"What the hell just happened?" Donovan asked. "I did everything—"

"You were perfect," Tess replied. "We didn't come here expecting him to attack me in the middle of the restaurant, right? Let's take our time driving home and see if anyone follows."

"Yeah," he replied, taking his shades off and unbuttoning his tuxedo jacket. "Anything?" he asked the driver.

"I can't see anyone trailing us," replied the driver, a special agent by the name of Osborne. He was one of the FBI regional bureau drivers, a former field agent, someone they could trust. Tess had rarely worked with him. After taking a bullet in the line of duty, he opted for a safer assignment; he was the single parent of a four-year-old son.

"So, where the hell is he?" Tess asked, frustrated. "I can't think of a better target than Finch and his new girl."

"Well, he isn't following us, that's for sure," SA Osborne replied.

Tess turned her head and looked behind. The street was entirely dark, not a single car was visible behind them.

She took out her phone and dialed Patto.

"Do you have him?" he asked, not even saying hello.

"No, we don't have the bastard," she replied, not bothering to hide her frustration. "What's going on with Mosley? Is he still okay?"

"All is fine here, Winnett. Nothing's happened."

"Then let's keep rolling," she decided after giving it a moment's thought. She had hoped the unsub would've stood out somehow at the restaurant, and she wouldn't have to lure him to her own place. "Maybe we get lucky later on. Who's my backup?"

"We have SSA Walz standing by at the rendezvous point, barely three blocks away from your house, and there's the two of us," SA Osborne replied. "We drop you off, turn the car around as if we're leaving, then come back within minutes in our tactical units, but approach carefully on foot. That was the original plan."

"Yeah, good, let's stick to it."

Tess looked behind again, hoping to see another car's headlights. The street was eerily dark.

Chapter 12

Donovan held her hand all the way to the front door where they exchanged one more loaded smile. She reached up to kiss him and he mumbled under his breath, still smiling, "Don't even think about it, Winnett."

She brought her lips even closer to his and whispered back, "Wouldn't cross my mind."

Then she pulled herself from the embrace, unlocked the door, and stepped inside.

She took a deep breath and pulled out her weapon, listening attentively for any sound that didn't belong. It was perfectly quiet, except for the limo door slamming shut and its engine purring as it drove away.

She turned on the hallway light, then kicked off her painful sandals with a satisfied groan, hand still firm on the handle of her Sig. She cleared the house carefully, one room after another, taking her time. She checked the back door and found it locked. When she finished her search, she headed into the dark living room and stared at the deserted street, gun still in hand.

She made sure no one could see her from outside if they looked. She kept the lights off, and the curtains closed.

No one was there. The unsub hadn't taken the bait.

He might've already been gone by the time Donovan and she arrived for dinner. He might've been circling Mosley's house like a vulture, trying to find his way in, aware his five weeks were about to run out.

What was more important for an unsub with his profile? Keeping true to his commitment to kill Mosley tonight? Or impulsively taking the bait of a new target and coming to finish her off?

The Word Killer hadn't proven patient or organized; he'd attacked without preparation, without studying or stalking the victims, leaving the crime scenes littered with DNA and fingerprints. His targets were ambitious though; he didn't go for high-risk victims like prostitutes or drug addicts; he went for low-risk targets from affluent circles, women and men surrounded by family, friends, colleagues, and, in some cases, staff.

Impulsive. Disorganized. Extremely violent.

Then, where the heck was he?

She sighed and decided to head into the bedroom and change into something more comfortable. There was no point in trying to wait for him in a backless dress that rode up her legs at every step. Gun still in hand, she headed into the kitchen first, pining for a glass of cold water.

She didn't hear him coming.

When he hit the back of her knees, she fell forward, her arms flailing, her knees hitting the floor hard, her gun flying out of her hand, across the room and under the dining room table. She saw stars and couldn't draw breath enough to scream. The second blow was aimed for the back of her head, but she'd wriggled and turned to face him. His boot found her shoulder, and she heard the bone crack.

Unwanted memories flooded her mind, seeding panic in her brain and illogical, disorganized responses in her behavior. She whimpered and begged, trying to erase the memory of the assault that had happened twelve years ago.

It couldn't happen again. Please, no.

The man laughed hysterically while undoing his belt buckle, and in that split second, she focused on his face enough to recognize him.

The restaurant host.

She recalled the long, admirative stare he'd given her, although he wasn't the only one. But his glance had felt different somehow, loaded with anticipation.

Because he knew he'd come for her.

And she'd missed it.

A sob escaped her throat as she pushed herself away from him, weak, dizzy, desperately expecting Donovan and the rest of the agents to kick the door down and end her pain.

He grabbed her ankle and pulled her toward him, and she screamed. She kicked him with both feet, and that got him laughing loudly, a raspy, insane laugh.

"Tell me about Delilah," she said, her eyes riveted on the hand lowering his zipper.

Stunned, he stopped and searched her eyes with a drilling stare. "You know about Delilah?"

She panted, trying to slow her breathing, her panic, and think. "Yes, I know her... She was beautiful, wasn't she?"

He slapped her across the face so hard she saw stars again. "What do you know about Delilah?"

Burning tears flooded her eyes, but she blinked them away and licked the blood off her swollen lip.

"I know you loved her," she replied, wishing more than anything that she'd be right in her analysis. "And she betrayed you."

He looked at her with hollow eyes. "She threw me away like I was nothing!" he bellowed. "Like I was a piece of trash."

A mother or maybe a lover, Tess thought, her mind racing with possibilities. Most likely a mother. But what was his trigger? What could've recently happened to make him relive the anguish of the original trauma, tenfold as painful and enraging?

"She had to be with him," she dared, shooting from the hip and holding her breath.

"And for what? For money, like the slut that she was!" he shouted. "She chose a life of luxury while I went from foster home to foster home, getting raped, used, and beaten."

He looked at her as if he'd never seen her before. She'd pushed herself away from him inch by inch, getting closer to the weapon that had slid under the table, almost within reach. She ventured a quick glance behind her, to gauge the distance to the gun, then looked straight at him with all the compassion she could muster.

What was the name he wore on his tag? There'd been so many... Richard. His name was Richard.

"You're a kind person, and you'd almost forgiven her," she said softly. "Because you still loved her. Until..."

Tess held her breath, sliding on her back one more inch, while the man stared into nothingness, into his own troubled past.

"What happened, Richard?" she asked softly.

He clenched his fists so violently his bones crackled. Involuntarily, Tess winced, anticipating a fatal blow. She eased herself farther away and extended her arm above her head, reaching for the Sig.

It was too far.

The man bellowed, then punched a hole in the wall next to him.

"She came into the restaurant one night, that piece of shit with her, and didn't even recognize me! He didn't recognize me either." He grabbed Tess by the neck and lifted her from the ground. "Can you believe it, Delilah? The man who didn't want your kid didn't even recognize me." He slammed her to the ground, laughing. "You're going to remember me now, Delilah. You'll like it."

"What happened to Delilah, Richard?" she asked, her voice trembling, shuttered with short gasps of air.

His eyes blurred, staring into empty space while his own past haunted him mercilessly.

"She left me…all over again. From the restaurant, she went to the airport and flew away. I—I lost her all over again." His hollow eyes focused on Tess's face again. "I found you now, Delilah, and this time, I won't let you go."

She reached around, desperate, and grabbed a vase from the table and hit him on the head with it. He didn't skip a beat. Instead, he flipped her on her stomach and pulled out a knife. She fought desperately to free herself while his hand came down with the blade.

Then she heard a shot. And another.

Richard fell next to her, blood dripping out of two chest wounds, quickly spreading onto the floor, about to reach Cat's boots.

He kicked the man's body away from her and extended his hand. She grabbed it, unaware of the tears streaming from her eyes. She sat by the killer's body, too shaken to risk getting to her feet.

Cat helped her up, then hugged her tightly, rocking her back and forth, the smoking .45 still in his hand.

"That's twice," she whispered, wiping the blood spatter from her face. "The second time you saved my life."

"Is he dead?" Cat asked, giving the fallen man a look. "If not, I can finish the—"

Tess crouched next to the body and checked for a pulse. "Yeah, he's dead."

"Great," Cat replied.

She looked at him and saw he looked scared. "You don't have a permit for this gun, do you?"

He lowered his eyes. "No... I'm not really someone who should talk to cops, in any capacity, if you catch my drift."

"Jeez, Cat," she said, then reached out and kissed his cheek. "I'll take care of this." She grabbed the gun from his hand. "Did you kill anyone else with this?"

"Just him," he replied, pointing at the body.

"Come on, get out of here," she said, patting his shoulder. "Go home, tell Danielle it's over."

Cat ran into Donovan, Walz, and Osborne on his way out the front door.

"What the hell?" Donovan reacted, not recognizing him.

"You schmucks are late," he groaned, giving them a dismissing stare. "The party's over."

Tess smiled widely, continuing to wipe the fingerprints off Cat's gun.

Donovan rushed inside, then stopped in his tracks when he saw the body lying in a pool of blood at Tess's feet.

"When did this happen? We were just around the corner to change cars."

"Doesn't matter, we got the guy," she replied, moving to unload the weapon and wipe the fingerprints off each bullet under their stunned eyes.

"The host, huh?" Donovan said. "How on earth did he find you?"

She turned toward Osborne, the smile still lingering on her lips.

"Did you leave the car while we were in the restaurant?"

"Only for two minutes," he said. "I had to use the restroom."

Tess pressed her lips together. "I'm willing to bet he put a tracker on the limo when you were gone."

Osborne's blood drained from his face. "I—I don't know what to say, SA Winnett. I'm so sorry."

She dismissed the apology with a hand gesture that brought a wince of pain to her face. "Don't worry about it. We got the guy. That's all that matters. That's what I'll put in my report."

She slid the bullets back into the magazine and started handling the gun to leave her own fingerprints on it.

"What's that?" Walz asked.

"My backup weapon."

"You carry a Colt 1911 as your backup weapon?"

"It's my dad's from 'Nam. I don't carry it. I keep it there, just in case," she replied, pointing at a two-shelf coffee table. "It hasn't been fired in ages."

They looked straight at each other for a while, then SSA Walz said, "Shouldn't be a problem, because we witnessed you shooting the suspect in self-defense. Over the years, many people might've handled, repaired, or cleaned that weapon; some before you were born."

She nodded almost imperceptibly. "Yeah, that's what I thought."

She let herself sink into the cushions of her couch and whimpered when the move kindled the pain in her shoulder.

"I'll get you an ambulance," Donovan said, and immediately made the call.

"Never mind that," she groaned. "What the hell am I going to do with that BCI Insurance case?"

"What insurance case?" Patto asked, walking through the

open door. "I heard you got the guy."

She pointed at the dead body, then turned to look at Patto with a blooming smile on her bruised lips. "Patto, you owe me one, don't you?"

He shook his head, frowning.

"Really, you do," she insisted, pointing at the body. "You see, I need a favor. There's this insurance fraud case... I'm sure you can dig up something and close it in no time."

Did *Not Really Dead* keep you riveted to the pages as you raced through the story, gasping at every twist? Find out what happens next for Tess Winnett and her team, in the next unmissable Leslie Wolfe thriller.

Read on for previews from

Girl with a Rose

A missing fifteen-year-old girl. A determined FBI Agent who has a terrible choice to make. A desperate race to catch a killer.

*** and ***

A Beautiful Couple

He's a charismatic TV anchor with everything to lose. She's the perfect wife, desperate to protect their life. But after one fatal mistake, their picture-perfect world starts to unravel.

Thank You!

A big, heartfelt thank you for choosing to read my book. If you enjoyed it, please take a moment to leave me a four or five-star review; I would be very grateful. It doesn't need to be more than a couple of words, and it makes a huge difference.

Join my mailing list to receive special offers, exclusive bonus content, and news about upcoming new releases. Use the button below, visit www.LeslieWolfe.com to sign up, or email me at LW@WolfeNovels.com.

Did you enjoy *Not Really Dead*? Would you like to see some of these characters return? Which ones? Your thoughts and feedback are very valuable to me. Please contact me directly through one of the channels listed below. Email works best: LW@WolfeNovels.com or use the button below:

If you haven't already, check out *Dawn Girl*, a gripping, heart stopping crime thriller and the first book in the Tess Winnett series. If you enjoyed *Criminal Minds*, you'll enjoy *Dawn Girl*. Or, if you're in a mood for something lighter, try *Las Vegas Girl*; you'll love it.

Connect With Me

Amazon.com/LeslieWolfe

LW@WolfeNovels.com

Amazon.com/stores/Leslie-Wolfe/author/B00KR1QZ0G

LeslieWolfe.com

Facebook.com/wolfenovels

Instagram.com/Wolfe.Leslie

TikTok.com/@Leslie.Wolfe

Bookbub.com/authors.leslie-wolfe

Preview: *Girl With A Rose*

1

Pose

She was thrilled she'd agreed to pose for him.

She almost hadn't made it past the imposing gates of the mansion, the likes of such she'd only seen in the movies. But the man had left a four-digit code scribbled with his address, and after fidgeting in place in front of the twelve-foot high, wrought-iron entrance, she noticed the keypad on a stand at the edge of the driveway, at the right height to be accessed from the driver's seat of a car. She'd entered the four digits with slightly trembling fingers, and the wrought iron set in motion, opening without a sound.

Mom would kill me if she knew where I'm at, she'd thought excitedly, her rebellion putting a spring in her step.

She'd walked the long, curvy driveway in a daze, taking in the beauty of the landscape with its fantastic rose bushes, each of them a different, exotic variety. She'd stopped a couple of times and buried her face in the dew-sprinkled blooms, taking in their aroma, savoring their intoxicating scent.

Then she rang the bell, while butterflies swarmed in her belly, and he opened the door almost immediately. He wore tight, worn-out jeans and a white T-shirt, both stained with paint, as were his arms and even his smiling face. She followed him inside, too intimidated to articulate a single word, her eyes riveted on the paintings that covered the walls of the living room. Beautiful girls, some sad, some playful, all young and innocent, their beauty enhanced by a single rose bloom.

Her step slowed and faltered as a strange sense of foreboding chilled her blood. She gazed quickly at the paintings again, this time searching the girls' eyes, looking for something, for a clue into what was to come, but their expressions remained mysterious, almost grim. The chill in her body turned to icicles streaming in her blood, and she let a quiet whimper escape her lips.

He turned and smiled, his smile warming the room. "What's wrong, my dear?"

She felt like an idiot. Posing for such an artist was a huge opportunity for her, and she was screwing it up as only she could. "Um, nothing, really," she managed, wringing her hands nervously and avoiding his deep, blue eyes. "All this," she gestured toward the walls covered in luxuriously framed canvases, "I—I don't know what to say."

"They're beautiful, aren't they?" he said, his voice filled with warmth as if the girls immortalized on canvas were all long-departed friends he dearly missed.

Then he turned toward her and widened his smile. "But they're gone… and you're here. You're even more beautiful, Kaylee."

Blood rushed to her cheeks, warming them quickly.

"When we're finished, I'll make room for you right here, above the mantle. You'll be my *pièce de résistance*," he added, the French words lending their charm to his already charismatic voice. His fingers brushed against her cheek for an instant, in a featherlight touch. "Your beauty is unique."

The last shadow of foreboding coldness left her body under his electrifying touch. She smiled timidly, painfully aware of how out of place she looked, of how childish her behavior was. She desperately wished she could instantly be a few years older and the kind of girl this man could fall in love with.

And she didn't even know his name.

She breathed and decided the woman he would like for more than a model for a painting would have the courage to ask his name.

"What, um, do I call you?" she managed, blushing again at the sound of her voice, strangled by emotion.

"David," he replied, searching her eyes and still smiling. "You can call me David." Then he turned to leave, looking at her over his shoulder. "Come on, we've got work to do, and we'll lose the light in a few hours."

She followed him eagerly through another couple of rooms, then entered his studio. An entire wall was made of glass panels, letting the sunshine in without restrictions. Through the large windows, she could see the exquisite garden in the back of the house, intricate alleys weaving between rose beds with blooms in various colors and shapes. Here and there, wooden benches under the shade of secular oaks or a fountain springing crystalline water on top of carefully arranged boulders.

It was as if she'd left the modern age at the wrought-iron gate and had entered the mansion of a nineteenth-century royal.

Surreal.

And it would make one hell of a story to tell Alice tomorrow. She'd have to share some of her adventures with her best friend, in return for her commitment to cover for Kaylee at school and with her mother, in case things would run late here and she'd call, all freaked out like Mom always got when she was even a minute past her curfew. School was easy, knowing how the Catholic prudes rushed to change the subject when any mention of cramps or other period-related issues were brought up, especially by a freshman. But her mom was another thing altogether; no mention of cramps would fly with her. *Being a teenager sucks*, she thought bitterly. *All day in school, then rushing home or else Mom throws a fit and grounds me forever, when I could be hanging out here, with a guy like that.*

"Don't," David said gently, touching her chin briefly to invite her to look at him.

"Huh?" she reacted, taken by surprise.

"You're frowning," he said, a tinge of disappointment in his voice.

She smiled apologetically and looked around for a place to sit.

There were a few pieces of furniture in the studio, scattered loosely on the vast floor in front of an easel holding a large canvas, all upholstered in black leather. A large armchair Kaylee could've easily curled up in, with her legs folded under her, and taken a nap. An inviting lounge chair that looked cozy and comfortable, the kind she'd seen only in fashion magazines. A bed, covered in red satin sheets and littered with pillows of all colors, the sight of which brought fire to her face. And a wide bench without a backrest, long enough to seat three, maybe four, people.

A new smile tugged at the corners of David's mouth as he followed her gaze.

"Let's seat you over here," he said, pointing at the bench.

She obeyed and sat, amazed at the softness of the leather under her touch.

"I brought some different clothes," she said, taking off her backpack.

"No need," he replied, his smile gone, replaced with an intense, scrutinizing look.

Her frown returned promptly. "You're painting me in my school clothes?" Her disappointment was raw, carrying the promise of tears.

"No, my dear," he replied, almost absentmindedly, ambling around her, studying her in detail. "This will be a head portrait."

"Oh," she whispered, feeling intimidated again under his scrutiny. Was her skin perfect? How about her hair?

"Did you remember to turn off your cell phone, like I asked? I don't like being interrupted while I work."

"Yes," she replied quickly, pulling it out of her pocket and showing him the dark screen.

"Good," he replied, then moved the easel a few feet to the right. He peeked from behind the canvas to look at her and then disappeared again for a few moments.

She heard his footsteps leaving the room, but she stayed in place, unsure of what to do. In his absence, the sense of foreboding returned, chilling her blood once again. There was a half-finished canvas leaned against the wall, the portrait of a girl holding a rose blossom to her lips, but her eyes looked haunted as if life was leaving her body. Kaylee's skin prickled with goosebumps, and she wrapped her arms around herself, shivering.

"It gets cold in here in the mornings," David said, startling her. She'd not heard him return, but he was there by her side, holding a steaming cup of tea. "The studio doesn't have heating, but the sun will do the trick." He offered her the cup. "It's chamomile with a touch of honey; it will help you relax."

She took the cup and, under his commanding gaze, took a sip. It was delicious, warming her body and scaring the apprehension away. She thanked him and sipped again, letting the thin vapor touch her face.

He walked over to a small table and brought back a tray, setting it on the bench by her side. Laid neatly on the tray were hairbrushes and combs, several fancy hairpins and accessories, scissors, and a few rose blooms in different shades of pink.

"May I?" he asked, picking up a hairbrush.

She shrugged. "Sure." She bit her lip, trying to hide her nervousness at the thought of him touching her. Yet strangely, she was disappointed he'd chosen pink blooms for her when the garden held stunning shades of crimson, purple, even blue with a yellow center. Pink was so banal.

He was gentle, removing her scrunchy without pulling her hair. Then he brushed it until it crackled with electricity, stopping a few times to evaluate the results of his work. Kaylee wished there was a mirror in the room, where she could see what she would look like after he was finished. She'd probably have to wait for the painting to be done to see her new image.

He set the hairbrush down and whispered, "Good." Then he lifted her hair up, strand by strand, weaving and arranging it in a high, braided updo pinned in place with a sophisticated, diamond-encrusted clip. Then he loosened a few thin strands around her face and arranged them carefully with his fingers, his face so close to hers she could feel his breath on her cheeks, sending shivers through her body.

He took a few steps back to admire his work, then let a quiet whistle sum up his conclusions.

She smiled widely. "Is there a mirror—"

His frown returned, digging deep ridges in his forehead. "No mirror, no. Please, be patient."

She lowered her gaze and took another sip of tea, a touch of uneasiness unfurling in her gut, a feeling she couldn't name, a warning she couldn't read.

He picked up a rose, then removed all its thorns with a pair of scissors. He trimmed the stem to four or five inches, then slid the stem behind her ear and secured the heavy bloom in place with two hair clips.

"We're ready," David said, rubbing his hands together, satisfied. "Finish your tea so we can get started."

She was happy to oblige, her throat feeling parched for some reason. She felt weak, almost trembling, and hoped the honey in the tea would pick her up a little and give her a touch of a sugar rush.

She set the empty cup on the bench near her, seeing more than feeling how badly her hand shook. His eyes lingered on her trembling hand, but he said nothing. He disappeared behind the canvas for a few moments and returned pushing a small cart with paint tubes, a small bowl, and a makeup kit like she'd never seen before. Only artists and musicians must've had a case like that, a silver suitcase that arranged in three levels when open, holding everything she could ever need if she were a star.

Dizzy and a little nauseated, she took her frozen hand to her forehead, hoping that the cold touch would make her feel better.

"Don't touch your hair," David commanded, his voice strong, almost angry.

She let her hand fall back into her lap. She tried to speak, but only a faint whimper came out. "I—I can't—"

"Here, lie down," he invited, supporting her head carefully with his hand until it touched the soft cushion of the bench. He slid a pillow under her head, then put her legs up on the bench with gentle, thoughtful moves.

He wasn't asking the right questions, wasn't calling an

ambulance. Her prior sense of foreboding had returned as sheer panic, but she couldn't scream, she couldn't move. She could still focus her eyes somewhat and watched every move he made while terror took over her heart, knowing what he'd done when he'd spiked her tea, but not understanding why.

"You must feel dizzy and numb right now," he explained patiently as if talking to a small child, "and that's normal. Well, maybe not to you, but I can assure you it's quite normal to me." He caressed her cheek, removing a rebel strand of thin, blonde hair. "I know you'd like me to say that everything will be all right, and it will be, but not for you, my dear. Not for you. Although you might enjoy what's coming."

He picked up a small porcelain bowl and held it above her face. "Do you know what this is? Bone ash porcelain. Human bones, burned to ash, are mixed in with the kaolin, to make the finest pieces of china there can be. The bones make the material stronger so that the porcelain can be thinner, almost translucent. See?"

She couldn't say a word. She tried, but no sound came out of her mouth, as panicked thoughts raced through her mind. What time was it? When would her mom freak out and call someone? A tear rolled down her cheek and disappeared in her hair. *Mom,* she called in her mind, *please find me. I promise I'll be good. I'll never lie to you again.*

She felt a pinprick in her arm and watched as David pierced her vein with a thin needle attached to a small plastic tube. Unable to lift her head, she could barely see what he was doing, but he'd elevated her arm on a couple of pillows, and she could catch a foggy glimpse.

Her blurry eyes locked on the blood leaving her body, in a steady string of droplets, collecting in the bone china bowl engraved with intricate gold leaves. She drew breath and let out a shriek that no one heard, not even her; no sound came off her parted lips.

He grinned and wiped her tears with cold fingers. "You mustn't cry, my dear. I'll apply your makeup next, and you're going to ruin it all."

Her heart fluttered frantically against her rib cage like a trapped bird fighting for its life, willing to smash itself against the bars rather than die at the hand of its captor. But all she could do was watch every move he made, unable to fight, unable to resist.

He mixed a few droplets of blood with paint from various tubes, adjusting the composition until it seemed perfect to him. Then he applied the paint on her lips, checking the crimson hue against direct sunlight and shade. He added a few droplets to some scrapings of eyeshadow on a tiny plate stained with dried paint, tinting the powder's hue to match the lipstick. She felt the applicator touch her eyelids gently, while his finger forced her eyes shut, one at a time.

"That's it," he exclaimed happily. "You're ready, my dear, and you are absolutely exquisite." He chuckled lightly, but then groaned and rushed to tap her cheek with a napkin. "No more crying, you hear me? You'll ruin everything."

He stared at her and licked his lips with anticipation, his charismatic smile turning into a grin filled with lust. He removed her clothing with ease, careful not to pull the needle out of her arm, then gave her young body one more appreciative look.

She tried to scream again; her desperate efforts, visible only in her eyes, bringing a lascivious smirk on his face.

"Scream all you want, my dear. I like you more when you're

feisty."

2

Missing

Tess typed her report quickly, a faint smile lingering on her lips. Only one feeling was more rewarding than the closing of a case with a neatly typed final report, all t's crossed and all i's dotted: when she actually caught her man. Or woman, for that matter, but most of the unsubs were men. That unique, adrenaline-injecting moment that made her blood rush through her veins while her heart thumped loudly in her chest, when she had the unsub in her sights, exposed, cornered, finished. What a rush!

Unfortunately, that moment had also proved to be the one when most chose to forge ahead against all logic and leave her no other option but to discharge her weapon. Her smile vanished as she typed that section of the report, while the words of her supervisor, Special Agent in Charge Pearson, resounded in her memory.

"You have the highest kill rate in the entire regional bureau, Winnett," he'd said. "You've been cleared in every incident, but you're under scrutiny, and all your future cases will be reviewed by the committee. For a while, at least, until you demonstrate you can actually slap a pair of handcuffs on a perp and give the Miami-Dade State attorney a reason to earn his keep."

SAC Pearson would probably be *thrilled* to read her latest report, just as she was to write it, early in the morning, way before the office floor got busy with traffic and loud with chatter and phones ringing. Her latest case had involved a drug-smuggling ring that had expanded into human trafficking, and she'd caught the ringleader in the act. She should've waited and called for backup, but there was a chance the girls he and his cronies were escorting off a powerboat would disappear into the ring's maze of safe houses and brothels, never to be seen again. Out of options, she'd pulled out her weapon and summoned him to surrender, silently begging him to surrender quietly. He'd grinned and lunged at her, gun drawn, and she'd tapped him in the chest. Twice.

She'd managed to arrest the two other perps, but still.

SAC Pearson must've been already fuming. She could feel it in the air, in the deathly silence engulfing the entire floor, in the sideways glances the few early risers threw her way when passing by her desk. SACs were the first notified whenever a weapon was discharged by one of their agents. He must've been already rapping his fingers against the desk, awaiting her report, growing angrier by the minute. He was there… she didn't imagine things. The light was on in his office, and the door wide open. Oh, well. *Que será, será.*

She nodded slowly while rereading her report, editing a word here and there. Her eyes lingered for a moment on the document's header.

FBI Case Report by SSA Tess Winnett

She'd recently earned a promotion, adding the second "S" to the acronym preceding her name. Now she was a supervisory special agent with the Federal Bureau of Investigation. A supervisory without a team. An SSA who'd probably never get a team assigned to her, and she was grateful for that. She loved her job just the way it was: a primal manhunt, twisted mind games played with the most chilling murderers out there, unencumbered by the complication of working with others. Teamwork had never been her strength. She loved the pursuit of justice, the ability to right the ugliest and most twisted, perverted, and sickening wrongs in her corner of the world. Each solved case filled her chest with swelling pride, even if at times chilled by the anticipation of SAC Pearson's reprimand because this time, yet again, her main perp was hosted in the morgue, not in lockup.

Her phone rang, and she was startled, then groaned as she read the name on the caller ID, right underneath the time stamp showing 6:43 A.M. in digital script.

"In my office, Winnett," Pearson said, without giving her the time to say anything. "Now."

She swore under her breath and hit the print command on her keyboard, then paced around the printer like a caged animal, impatient to see all twelve pages come out of the machine. Then she grabbed them and the case folder and rushed out toward Pearson's office, without taking the time to arrange the pages and staple them together.

She found Pearson looking out the window with a sad expression on his face, and before he beckoned her in, she caught a glimpse of a black-and-white photo on his desk. It showed a much younger, slimmer Pearson, who still had hair on his head and knew how to smile, by the side of a determined, athletic woman, probably another FBI agent.

Tess handed Pearson the case file, but he gestured toward the pile on his desk and then invited her to take a seat.

"There's a missing persons case I'd like you to look into," he said, his eyes still riveted to the cityscape visible outside his window.

"Sure," she replied, wondering which miracles had aligned to work in her favor and help her skip past the chewing out she'd been expecting.

"It's a kid," he added with a barely contained sigh. "A fifteen-year-old girl."

"Fifteen?" she reacted. The FBI usually investigated missing or kidnapped children age twelve or younger, and there was a specialized response team for that, the Child Abduction Rapid Deployment Team, or CARD. When a fifteen-year-old went missing, there usually had to be local police involvement and a request for assistance was expected before the bureau would engage. "Which county called us in?"

Pearson hesitated for a split second, enough time for his expression to shift slightly, becoming more focused. He turned and looked straight at her.

"Do this as a personal favor to me, Winnett, will you?" He sounded pained, worried.

"Sure," she replied. "I'll need some details to get started." She took a small notebook out of her pocket and grabbed a pen from his desk.

He sat behind the desk, the chair grumbling under his massive frame. He stared for a moment at the photo of his younger self and the unknown woman, then rubbed his forehead as if fighting a silent migraine.

When he finally spoke, his tone was the one Tess knew well: firm, uncompromising, factual.

"Kaylee Lewis, fifteen, was last seen yesterday evening, when she left her friend's house, heading home. Both girls go to school at Bayshore High."

Tess whistled. That was one of the most expensive private schools in the area.

"There's a catch, Winnett," he added. "The last person to see Kaylee was Alice, her best friend. Alice Bachert is her full name."

Tess sprung to her feet. "The governor's kid?"

"Yes," Pearson said. "Sit down, Winnett."

"Are you setting me up, sir?" she asked, before she could realize what she was saying and to whom.

"Jeez, Winnett! Are you serious right now?"

"The governor asked you twice to get rid of me," she replied quickly, feeling the blood rush to her head. "Do you think I can waltz into his house and question his daughter?"

"Yes. You're the only one who can."

That answer left her slack-jawed and at a loss for words. She sat and waited for Pearson to say more.

"Bachert called me twice about you, in each case demanding your badge for bothering his friends. But you didn't care. You still closed those investigations successfully, while most agents would've considered the impact an enemy like the pissed-off governor of the state of Florida could've had on their careers."

"Oh, I see," she replied. "I'm now officially qualified fodder for the governor's shitfits," she mumbled.

"No, Winnett. You're the only agent in this regional office with a one hundred percent case close ratio. You have an open position waiting for you with Behavioral Analysis in Quantico that you refuse to accept, but it's still kept open, nevertheless. You're the best agent I can think of, the only one I trust with Kaylee's life. You don't care about politics and will bring Kaylee back to her mother at any cost."

"What about Bachert? He had it in for me when it was only about his friends being bothered with a few questions. Do you think sending me to his house to speak with his own kid is the best approach? This can go wrong in any number of different ways."

Pearson sighed, his patience running to a visible low. "Yeah, he'll call, and he'll complain, and he'll demand we fire you like he's done before. That doesn't mean we'll do that. Give us some credit, will you?"

She wasn't going to give *them* much credit, whoever *they* were. Maybe she'd give Pearson some credit, yes, considering he could've already fired her but had obviously decided against it. However, in her many years with the bureau, she'd seen politics in action before, turning friends into enemies and honest agents into backstabbers for far less. However, all Bacherts of the world aside, there was a kid missing, albeit for only a few hours. Screw that short-fused, entitled asshole.

"You could also choose to go easy on him, be polite, respectful, show some courtesy instead of your typical bluntness," Pearson added.

She frowned and glared but managed to refrain from adding she wasn't going to kiss a politician's rear end just to make him or Pearson happy.

"Let's talk about Kaylee," she replied instead. "Are we sure this kid didn't choose to go on a date that went a little long? Did the county log in her case as a missing person?" she asked, although she knew the answer. Police don't log a missing person's report in the first hours since they were last seen, it's usually after twenty-four hours.

"The mother called the police last night about eleven, but they haven't started an official investigation yet, and haven't called us in," he replied. He pushed the photo toward her and tapped his finger against its weathered surface. "Jennifer was my partner. An excellent agent, who taught me a lot of what I know today. Kaylee's mom is Jennifer's younger sister, Deanne. And Kaylee is my godchild," he added with a sad smile.

Tess wondered where the sadness was coming from. Kaylee

had barely gone missing, if she even was. Statistically, there was a good chance the girl would soon show up at home, begging her mother for forgiveness and swearing she'd never do it again. "How come Jennifer's not looking into this?"

"She was killed in the line of duty, almost ten years ago, in the same shootout that killed Kaylee's father. He was DEA."

"Oh," Tess whispered. She couldn't begin to imagine what Deanne and her daughter must've gone through that day, having to bury not one, but two loved ones. "Then we'll look into this ourselves. Why does her mother believe she's missing, as opposed to being inexcusably late?"

"Deanne called everyone she could think of, and no one has heard from her daughter after she left the Bachert residence about six. No texts, no Facebook, nothing. And she told me Kaylee's been different lately. New habits, new music, new clothes."

"Also known as being a teenager," Tess replied.

"That was my reaction too, but then Deanne said something I had to take seriously. She said she had a strong gut feeling about this."

"A parent's anxiety? That's all we have?"

"Kaylee's phone is off, and she's never broken the dusk curfew before." Pearson stopped for a moment, probably considering how unrealistic and thin his arguments were. "Kaylee's a good kid, Winnett. It's not like her to just vanish."

"A teenager with a dusk curfew?" She tried to refrain a smile. "How long was that going to last?"

"Okay, Winnett, you don't trust Deanne's gut. She's someone you've never met, in your mind just a scared, frantic parent fearing the worst. But do you trust *my* gut?"

Her smile vanished, and the answer came easily to her.

"With my life." In almost twelve years of working with him, Pearson had never been wrong. Not even once.

"Then believe me when I say, this girl's missing. She could've been taken, or just… something could've happened to her. This is Miami, Winnett, not a midwestern town where no one ever locks their doors."

"All right, that's good enough for me," she replied. "I'm assuming no ransom calls have been made yet?"

"None."

"I'll handle this angle too, just in case." She paused, checking her notes. "Deanne is a single mother, yet Kaylee is enrolled at a very expensive school. Is everything above water there?" She saw Pearson's frown and added, "I mean no disrespect. But if we have gang activity here, or some drug connection, I need to know."

"Deanne is a dentist with her own practice. I also happen to know that Kaylee's tuition is covered by her paternal grandparents, both retired attorneys."

Tess flipped the notebook shut. "That explains it," then checked her watch briefly. "She's been missing a little over twelve hours. We're still in the first twenty-four, but I'll drop everything and head out straight for the lion's lair."

"Huh?" Pearson reacted, looking up from Tess's latest case file.

"My good old friend, the governor. I'm heading out there now. I want to catch everyone while they're still at home. Expect your phone to start ringing. The man just hates my guts."

She stood, while Pearson looked at her intently, irritated at first, then almost pleading.

"For heaven's sake, Winnett, a kid's missing, do your damn

job already."

Offended, she took a couple of steps back. "Of course, I'll do my job; just saying there will be damage control left for you to clean up, sir."

Pearson glared at her without a word.

She turned and walked briskly out of his office, then shouted from the hallway, "And I'll need Donovan."

3

A Rose

Tess checked the time as she rushed toward Donovan's desk. He'd just arrived and was setting up for his day at the office. A large, transparent plastic travel mug with water and floating pieces of fruit came out of his backpack and landed on a coaster next to his keyboard. He held a smaller, paper cup, filled with coffee to the brim, taking small sips every second or so, while he fired up his computers.

An amazing analyst and a frustrated professional at the same time, Donovan tried every year for field agent and was rejected, also every year. The reason remained a mystery, at least for Tess. She'd probed with Pearson a couple of times, but he'd cut her curiosity off without disclosing any information. It could've been because the tall, broad-shouldered man lacked some critical skill needed in the field, or because he was so darn good at what he did that the regional bureau couldn't begin to imagine the workplace without Donovan as a technical analyst.

"Ah, the highlight of my day has just materialized," Donovan said in lieu of a greeting.

Or it could've been his manners. Cynical, dismissive at times, rushed, and usually sarcastic, coming across as arrogant to the bone, Donovan bristled almost everyone he worked with.

"Good morning to you too," Tess replied, unfazed. "We have an urgent missing persons case I need your—"

"Pearson's mystery kid?"

"It's not his kid, D, it's his godchild," she sighed. "And yes.

Her name is Kaylee Lewis."

Donovan's monitors were all lit up. He abandoned the coffee cup with a regretful look and sat in front of them, ready to type.

"Tell me what you need."

"I need ransom call and tracing deployed at the Lewis residence."

His fingers still lingered, immobile, above the keyboard.

"Done. I wasn't the only one Pearson woke up before the alarm clock."

She didn't bother to set him straight but felt a pang of frustration that her boss had called her analyst before he'd called her.

"Did you run a trace on the girl's phone?"

"The phone's off and hasn't pinged the network since yesterday at 12:37 P.M. Still waiting to hear back on the last known location."

She checked the time again and groaned.

"Too late now to rush to the governor's house. I'll interview Kaylee's mother first, then her best friend." She frowned as she considered her options. "Could you please call the Bachert residence and let them know I'm coming? I'll need Alice to be available to answer questions about Kaylee."

"Nice, Winnett," he grinned with clenched teeth. "Use me to handle that hot potato."

"He won't say anything to you," she replied. "He'll save it all for me."

She drove with lights and siren on to the Lewis residence, wondering why the girl had turned off her phone in the middle of a school day. Most kids spent their entire lunch breaks with their faces buried in the devices, preferring to text their friends instead of actually speaking with them, even if they're seated at the same table.

She found the residence easily. It was the only house on the quiet Bayshore street with three black SUVs parked in front, all with government plates. She recognized a couple of technicians from the bureau and greeted them, getting out of their way as they hauled call tracking and recording equipment. Within minutes, the technicians finished setting up, and two of the SUVs drove away, leaving behind a junior agent by the name of Gabriel Mendoza to pace the dimly lit living room with a wireless headset around his neck, waiting for the ransom call.

"Hey, Mendoza," she greeted him in a low whisper. "Where's—?"

He gestured with his head and she followed the direction of his glance. Deanne sat in the corner of the couch, crying softly. She must've sensed Tess approaching, because she looked up, then sprung to her feet.

"Have you heard anything?" she asked Tess, wiping her tears with the back of her hand.

"Nothing yet," Tess replied, and her two words sent a shockwave through the woman's body.

She sat, her feet seemingly too weak to sustain her.

"I have a few questions for you," Tess said. "Tell me about Kaylee. What's she like?"

"She's a wonderful kid," Deanne replied. "It's been just the two of us since her dad died, and she's strong and sweet, a good student." She sniffled, then looked at Tess with pleading eyes. "This isn't like her, to just disappear. You have to believe me. She'd never do that to me."

"I understand," Tess replied. The woman had given her almost zero useful information. Who was Kaylee as a person? Sometimes parents are the last to know when their children grow up and become individuals with entirely different, secret lives.

"Tell me about her friends." She decided to take a structured approach to the interview. "Who does she spend her time with?"

"Alice. Everything Kaylee does is with Alice, and I couldn't be happier about it. Alice is a nice girl, and her family is, well, the governor's family, so Kaylee spends a lot of time at their house. I know she's safe there. They study together, go to camp together, they've been inseparable since they were little," Deanne said, putting her hand in the air about three feet from the ground.

"Anyone else? Is there a boyfriend?"

"There is, or was, I should say," Deanne replied hesitantly. "Kaylee went out a couple of times with this boy from school, Jeremy Gafford. But now that you asked, I realize she hasn't been talking about him much lately. She tells me everything, my little girl," Deanne added, wiping a fresh tear off her cheek. "My days are long at the clinic, but dinners are a sacred ritual for my daughter and me. We talk about our day, laugh a little, and I try hard not to ask too much about schoolwork. She's an A student, you know."

Tess repressed a frustrated groan. She'd seen it many times before, when parents couldn't provide much insight into their children's interests and routine.

"How about her phone? Do you check your daughter's social media and texts?"

"Um, no... I respect her privacy and give her some freedom, more each year," Deanne replied, a hint of worry in her eyes.

For a brief moment, Tess considered whether to tell Deanne how wrong that was, in a world filled with psychopaths and pedophiles preying on children through social media. Maybe it wasn't the right moment to seed more fear in the poor woman's heart.

"What does Kaylee like?" she asked instead.

Deanne's face lit up. "She's into fashion a lot, always watching fashion shows and following supermodels on the internet. She is very particular about her looks, almost a little vain," she added, her voice tinged with guilt. "She accessorizes better than I do, and picks my own attire, because I'm just too busy to care much these days."

The statement rang true; Deanne wore simple, beige slacks and a white shirt.

She stood and invited Tess to follow her to the hallway, where framed photos showed Kaylee at various ages, always perfectly dressed, smiling with perfectly aligned, white teeth, her makeup impeccable.

Deanne being a dentist, the perfect dentition was to be expected. But the makeup? What age did teenage girls start using makeup these days?

"May I see her room?" Tess asked, and Deanne led the way.

Kaylee's bedroom was nothing Tess expected. Where teenagers lived, there usually was clutter, as if tornadoes routinely swirled everything in the air and then let objects fall to the ground where they happened to land. Kaylee's room was neat, the bed made impeccably with throw pillows arranged symmetrically and a plush teddy bear leaning against the middle pillow. Not a single sock, shoe, or clothing item lay scattered anywhere in sight. Curious, Tess opened the closet and found the same rigorous order ruling the countless clothes hangers and folded items.

Kaylee's room seemed ready for a fashion magazine layout

shoot. The rest of the house, however, seemed lived in.

"Who makes the bed?" Tess asked. "Do you have a housekeeper?"

"We have a service that comes every two weeks for major cleaning," Deanne said, sounding embarrassed. Probably, in the ritzy Bayshore area, it was inconceivable not to have a full-time maid. "But no, Kaylee makes her bed like that, every morning. And cleans up perfectly."

Tess frowned, but chose not to ask Deanne if she thought that behavior was normal for a teenager.

"She wants everything to be perfect," Deanne explained, understanding Tess's unspoken question. "She's a little vain, you know. I believe she might be competing with Alice somehow. You know, the governor has three permanent house staff, and everything is perfect in their household. Probably Kaylee doesn't want to be embarrassed when Alice visits."

"Makes sense," Tess conceded, although it didn't. Not really.

She opened a few desk drawers and examined the items neatly organized. Writing instruments in one, books and notepads in another. Then she went to the closet again and started opening drawers. At the far end of a sock drawer, she found an Estée Lauder makeup kit that must've been expensive. She pulled it out and opened it, while Deanne stared at it in disbelief.

"I didn't know she had this," she whispered. "I sometimes put a bit of makeup on her when we're going out or something. But I thought—" Her words trailed off as she covered her mouth with her hand.

"Most girls hide their makeup," Tess replied, studying Kaylee's clothing closely. Some of the items were expensive, but not beyond what a dentist mom could afford. "You bought her all these clothes?"

Deanne looked at the stacked closet closely. "Um, I recognize most of them, so, yes, I believe I did. Some are hand-me-downs, clothes I used to wear when I was younger."

Tess slid the closet door shut and returned near the bed. A couple of magazines were laid on the night table, again an unusual choice for a girl Kaylee's age. *American Art* and *Artists*, both recent issues and both showing signs of repeated use.

"Is Kaylee into art?" Tess asked, looking at the walls decorated with the typical band posters that teenagers liked. There was no art; Kaylee was a fan of Twenty One Pilots and Imagine Dragons.

"Not until recently," Deanne replied, frowning impatiently when Tess sat on the edge of the bed with the latest issue of *American Art* open in her lap.

Tess flipped through the pages carefully, wondering what Kaylee's interest could've been. Her interest must've been major, because the subscription, per the discount coupon included in the magazine's pages, was not cheap.

The pages gave off a fine scent, a whiff of high-end cologne, or some other scented cosmetic. She closed her eyes and inhaled, trying to identify the mysterious smell. Shower gel, maybe? *No, it's aftershave*, she concluded silently. That magazine did not come straight from the newsstand.

"Do you really have time for this?" Deanne snapped, her voice angry, her eyes filled with tears.

Tess stood, abandoning the magazine on the bed. "My only chance to find your daughter and bring her back to you is to understand who she is, what makes her tick."

Deanne shook her head. "I already told you…"

"Who is she, really? How would a predator approach her?

What would he lure her with? If she's a little vain and into fashion, would someone offer her a modeling audition?"

Deanne wailed, bending over with her hands clutched at her chest, as if the cry ripped her apart.

Great work, Winnett, always ready to put your foot in your mouth, Tess admonished herself for her bluntness.

She gently touched Deanne's shoulder.

"I promise you, I'll do everything in my power to find your daughter. And I'm not alone. I have resources, Pearson and the entire team are behind this investigation and we're not stopping until we find her."

Deanne straightened her back and looked Tess straight in the eye. "Find my baby... please. I—I can't think that someone took her... has her. I just... can't."

Kaylee had been gone more than twelve hours, and the absence of a ransom call was a bad sign. She could've been anywhere... snatched off the streets of Miami by human traffickers, to be shipped to who knows where and forced into prostitution. She'd just put a human trafficking ringleader into the ground, but probably by now three more had taken his place.

Kaylee could've been grabbed at random by a predator or lured by a stalker. She could've been attacked in the street and left bleeding in some alley. Regardless of the scenario, Kaylee's time was running out fast. The first twenty four hours were critical; after that, the chances of finding a missing person alive plummeted, and the most likely scenario would be finding her body. Those were the odds. If Alice had told the truth, Kaylee had last been seen at six P.M. the night before; almost fifteen hours.

Instead of sharing her thoughts, Tess held the woman's gaze

with a determined, reassuring look. "I promise," she replied. "Kaylee's one of ours, and we *will* find her."

Tess turned to leave, but another object caught her eye. A single, long-stemmed rose in perfect pink bloom, in a thin crystal vase, arranged tastefully at the center of a dresser. Not the usual fifteen-year-old bedroom décor.

"When's her birthday?" Tess asked.

"Kaylee turned fifteen almost a month ago."

"And this?" Tess pointed at the rose. "Secret admirer?"

A faint, sad smile fluttered on Deanne's lips. "She's not like that, I wish you'd believe me. No… this came from her best friend, Alice. She does these things sometimes."

Alice again.

Like *Girl With A Rose*?

Preview: *A Beautiful Couple*

1

AMANDA DAVIS

I killed a man.

The surreal words fill my mind, echoing in shock and fear with tremors that weaken my body. As reality starts setting in, I gasp silently, covering my mouth with a trembling hand, stifling a sob. Wide-eyed, I stare at the body lying in a motionless heap at the bottom of the stairs, disbelief clinging to me in scattered thoughts and anxious breaths.

It can't be true. He can't be dead.

But I can see it's all too real. In his neck, twisted and crooked sideways in an impossible posture. In the sickening crack of broken bones I remember hearing just as he was landing on the hardwood floor after bouncing down the steep flight of stairs. In the pooling blood that's slowly seeping from his head, gleaming burgundy under the yellowish light coming from the floor lamp by the door.

A noise outside makes me jump out of my skin. Someone's coming. I freeze in place at the top of the stairs, my fingers white-knuckled on the handrail, as the footsteps draw closer. Then, in the dark frame of the living room window, the profile of a woman appears, her face dimly lit as she passes by. Without turning her head to look inside.

I breathe.

Then I realize someone could've seen what happened. A passerby. A neighbor. Anyone.

I force some air into my lungs to steel my fraught nerves. Still holding on to the handrail for support, I climb down the stairs, careful not to slip, as if his fall could repeat somehow and seal my fate in vengeful symmetry, my body next to his. I hold my breath as I approach, senselessly hoping he's still alive, yet fearing it. When I eventually breathe, the metallic smell of blood fills my nostrils, filling me with dread.

I rush to the window and close the blinds, then peek outside between two slats. The street is eerily deserted and still. For now.

Crouching by his side, I feel for a pulse with frozen fingers. Touching his skin sears me, prickling the back of my head as if he could snap out of death and grab my shaky wrist.

There's no pulse.

His golf shirt is soaked with blood at the collar and smells faintly of aftershave, although his face shows a two-day stubble. His skull is fractured where it must've hit the edge of a step, the indentation clearly visible through his buzz-cut hair despite the bleeding laceration. Reluctantly, I slip my fingers and trace his neck, wincing as I find the protruding vertebra, a sign of a fractured cervical spine resulting in a fatal spinal cord injury.

He died the moment he hit the floor.

I'm more than qualified to make that statement. It doesn't change how I feel, though. Unsure of myself. Scared. Unsteady. My heart is racing, and my chest is tightening, as if the walls of this room are drawing closer and closer, about to squeeze the life out of me.

The sound of an approaching car makes me rush to the window and peek outside. It doesn't slow down until it reaches the corner and turns, tinting the darkness with hues of bright taillight red.

I turn on my heels and stare at the body, unsure what to do.

His eyes are still open, as if looking straight through me with hypnotizing, dilated pupils. It chills the blood in my veins. Barely touching him with the tips of my fingers, I crouch down and close his eyelids swiftly, shaking, eager to put some distance between me and him. I stand quickly and step back, feeling for the handrail, unable to take my eyes off of him. Part of me still expects him to get up and grab me, slam me against the wall, then put his hands around my throat and squeeze until my world goes dark. Just as his is now.

But he doesn't move. He's dead.

I killed him.

The enormity of what I've done weighs heavily on my heart. How could I let this happen?

It seems I had no choice, and yet, the truth is I *had* a choice, and I made the wrong one. That didn't happen a few moments ago, when I pushed him down the stairs.

No.

It happened earlier. Much earlier.

And now, I have to deal with the consequences of what I've done.

My first thought is to run, to put as much distance as I possibly can between me and the body lying on the blood-soaked floor. But there's no running away from this. Not right now. Not without a plan.

Still walking backward, my heel stops against the bottom step of the staircase and I nearly trip. I let myself slide down and sit on a step. For a moment of respite, my elbows rest on my shaky knees and my face lands in my hands, hiding from the grim sight.

Perhaps I could stall things for a few days before they come for me, because I know they will. Clinging to that glimmer of hope, my mind starts working. I raise my weary head and look around, taking inventory of everything I could use to buy myself some time. There isn't much.

One thing's certain: I have to get rid of the body.

That's when I realize I need help.

He's massive, at least six-three and well-built, weighing perhaps two-forty or about that much. It's what I liked about him... the strength, the agility, the apparent stamina and self-confidence. However, I'm not nearly that tall, and I'm one-forty at the most, on a bad, bloated day. I reach for his leg to test my strength, but stop before touching his ankle. It's pointless to even try. At work, it takes six of us to transfer a patient his size from the stretcher onto the bed.

I take out my phone and turn it on. The bitten apple lights up white on the black screen, then vanishes, making room for a picture of my son. Tristan just turned nine; we took that pic last summer, on the Santa Monica Pier. Seeing his piercing blue eyes touched by his enchanted smile brings the threat of tears to my eyes.

What if I lose him? What if they lock me up and I never see him again?

I can't bear the thought of that; it guts me. *No... I can't lose my son. It won't happen. Whatever it takes.*

I push the grim thoughts away and breathe deeply while putting in the passcode. His face disappears off the screen.

It will be all right. But the words I tell myself fail to reassure me.

As the screen fills with apps, I realize there's only one person I can call for the kind of help I need. The one person I'd rather never call or see again. My fingers falter retrieving the name from the contacts list. Hesitating, I give the fallen body another look, desperately wondering if there's any other way.

There isn't.

I brace myself for the questions that are about to come my way like machine gun bullets, merciless and cold and ripping through me in rapid-fire sequence.

Then I make the call, knowing that as soon as I share what I've done, there will be no turning back. My entire existence will be at the mercy of someone else. Someone I know I can't trust.

As the line rings in my ear, I reflect bitterly on the last few weeks, on everything that's happened.

I never wanted any of this.

All I wanted was a stupid divorce.

2

PAUL DAVIS

Two weeks ago

Hot damn. Tits like those should be illegal.

I touch my tie knot briefly, wishing I could loosen it a little. Instead, I end up straightening it—a reflex when I know I'm directly in camera view. Only, there's no camera trained on me. Not yet.

The cameras are all huddled outside the ballroom, where the guests keep arriving in their fancy cars and rental limos to attend the annual *Citizens Against Impaired Driving* fundraiser I'm chairing. Even so, I should be focusing on the people seated at the table with me, including my wife Amanda. But no...I can't focus on any of them.

Only on her, the stranger who captured my interest the moment we arrived at the venue. She's walking across the atrium with a sway of her hips, so rhythmic and smooth that it's as if she's dancing her way through to the light music in the background. Her satin gown hugs her perfect shape, taut over her perky, little breasts. A high leg slit lets me put eyes on more of her skin than my wife would appreciate. Good thing Amanda's not looking at me right now. She's chatting with an older woman seated next to her while I get to feast my eyes on the unsuspecting stranger.

The woman doesn't look my way, and I'm not used to being ignored. To feeling invisible. I hate how it makes me feel. I almost want to shout, "Hey, I'm here," but there's no point. I'd make an ass of myself. As she makes her way to the open bar, she turns away, and I can see that gown is a backless wonder, seemingly clinging only to her shoulders...and so lightly, I could make it fall off of her with the touch of a finger. The thought unsettles me. I shift in my seat. And keep watching.

Her back is just as perfect as everything else she's strutting. The dress, a deep shade of red, shimmers under the dim lights, generously draped and still tight over her ass. It dips daringly below the small of her flawless back. I can't keep my eyes off her.

I bet she's not wearing anything underneath that thing. For a moment, I imagine how it would feel to touch her smooth, glowing skin. How that perfectly shaped back would arch when I took her from behind. How she'd look at me after, laying spent on crumpled sheets, with her wavy, chestnut hair spread on my pillow.

She disappears from sight as a couple of men trail after her and block my view. They're probably sucked in by her wake, empty drink glasses in hand and following her like panting dogs on the prowl. I'm about to down my drink and give myself a reason to visit the open bar where she's headed, but my glass freezes in mid-air when I notice Amanda's eyes, drilling into me with barely contained rage.

She leans toward me until her breath touches my skin. "Really, Paul?" she whispers in my ear, faking a smile for whoever might be looking at us just now. "With me here? With all these people watching?"

My teeth grit as I set my glass down. I hate being scolded like I'm four. "I didn't do anything," I growl back in a low voice, hating myself for saying it, for making excuses. She doesn't reply. Just sits there smiling, pretending everything is okay, but her chest is heaving, and her lower lip is trembling slightly.

But I'm still angry.

I'll admit I can get pissed off easily.

I take a sip of bourbon to hide the emotion, and pretend to pay some attention to what an overly bejeweled, middle-aged woman across the ten-person table is telling me. But it's pointless; I'm too frustrated to care. She goes on and on about a nephew of hers who died, and I'm forced to sit here, nod, and take it. She makes sweet eyes at me, and I fear I'll be throwing up in my mouth soon. I wash away the bad taste with more bourbon, then continue to smile and nod every now and then as she tells her endless story. Soon enough, she'll write me a check.

That's why I'm here, for the *Citizens Against Impaired Driving* annual fundraiser, gracefully hosted in the university atrium. The vast room is lavishly decorated with cascading white flowers set on every ten-person table, placed at the center of fine, white table linen. We're seated on dressed-up chairs tied up with satin ribbons. The myriad lights are dimly shining above us from chandelier-like, modern LED fixtures featuring intricate layers of crystal-clear prisms that glimmer in flickers of rainbow. These are not the drab, fluorescent university atrium lights I remember from my prior visits. They must've had them replaced for tonight. They really went over the top this time. I'm impressed.

The sound of my wife's laughter catches my attention. She looks beautiful tonight, with her long, blond hair done perfectly so, and she captures the undivided attention of at least two men. And I'm supposed to be okay with that. As if she can read my mind, her hand lands on my forearm. I pull away, instinctively, the thought of being seen as my wife's attachment bothering me on a deep level.

The air hums with low-key chatter and the occasional drunken burst of laughter. Because, of course, what's more fitting for a sobriety organization event than an open bar?

The event is sponsored generously and advertised for free by Golden State Broadcasting, the TV station I work for. They make sure that all invitation-only attendees can afford to fork out at least a couple grand for the four-course gourmet meal and said open bar. And the privilege to mingle with television people and the few Hollywood stars in attendance, and perhaps get a selfie with someone famous.

And as the president of *Citizens Against Impaired Driving* for the past few years, I'm at the center of all of it, soon to take the stage for the final speech of the evening, as soon as the guests finish their desserts.

Yet, I'm annoyed as fuck.

My boss, Raymond Cook, the president and CEO of Golden State Broadcasting, is a balding bundle of blundering ego. This year, the fourth in the pained history of his favorite event, he decided that the most prominent people in the station be seated with random donors, to engage them in conversation and have them imbibing and star-struck by the time they sign those checks. For what it's worth, he was fair; he's seated with donors, too. But he doesn't have unfuckable women drooling all over him while his wife is seated by his side. And that's not because he's not married. It's because no one really knows who Raymond Cook is. And no one cares.

But Paul Davis? That's a different story.

3

PAUL DAVIS

I'm the face of the evening news and the brains behind it. I'm the lead anchor, and there's a reason for that. On the evenings I'm working, the Nielsen ratings go up, ad revenue climbs by at least ten percent, and viewership and engagement both spike. Yes, I'll admit that the spike is mostly reflecting women, and I'm secretly pleased with it.

With ratings like that, I got my own show two years ago. It's a fifteen-minute interview attached to the end of the news program, called *The Final Question*. There's no co-anchor involved; just me and whomever I choose—carefully—to skewer or commend that evening, dealer's choice. The show's been quite successful, further increasing the station's ratings. That's why Raymond Cook decided I should report directly to him. It was an actual promotion and came with more money— lots more money. Unfortunately, it also came with a closer working relationship between Raymond and me.

I'm not that happy about that part.

I hate his guts, and I'm sure he envies my popularity, although his bottom line loves it. Regardless of how I might feel about it, though, he's still the boss. He gets to call the shots. All of them. And never lets me forget it.

But that's not the only fly in my bourbon.

My former co-anchor, Carly Crown, is seated at my right. She's stunningly elegant in a sapphire blue dress with a plunging neckline that draws the immediate attention of every male in the room. Some females, too. Her blond hair is styled in loose waves and, tonight, looks disturbingly like my wife's. Perhaps she didn't intend it to, but I wouldn't put it past her. Every now and then, her knee rubs against my thigh.

I usually like the seemingly casual interactions, the not-so-accidental touching, the innuendo coloring our conversations at work. But not tonight. Not with a pissed off Amanda seated at my left. I don't want trouble on the home front.

Pulling away, I shoot Carly a warning glance. She veers her eyes toward the empty stage, but there's a certain tension in her lips that tells me I'm going to hear about my distance real soon. And I'm not going to like it. Carly is a death hazard dressed in Pierre Cardin.

The woman across the table stops speaking mid-phrase as the lights in the atrium grow brighter. Raymond climbs onto the stage and grabs the microphone. The light music in the background fades. He clears his voice and coughs into his fist—thankfully, before the mic goes live.

"Thank you all for being here with us tonight in beautiful Malibu. What a fantastic setting for such a noble cause! I hope you enjoyed the delicious meal as much as I did—though I must admit, the dessert might've been a bit too good. If I don't fit into my tux tomorrow, I'll know who to blame!"

The room regales him with a roar of laughter. I can tell the open bar made a difference this year.

"But before the evening comes to an end, there's the moment you've all been waiting for." He pauses for a moment, and the audience stills.

About fucking time.

We've been doing this for four years, and this is the first time he's letting me speak. I straighten my tie knot once more, but refrain from smoothing my hair with my hands. I'm ready.

No, I'm not. I take another sip of bourbon. *Now, I am.*

"She saves lives for a living," Raymond says, gesturing at and looking in Amanda's direction. The limelight follows his lead and finds us. My wife smiles shyly and bows her head. "As a critical care nurse working the endless battlefields of impaired driving, she's the first one to see the carnage. She will tell you that not everyone makes it, even if Sunset Valley Medical Center's Trauma Unit is one of the best in the nation. She has witnessed, time and again, the heartbreak a split-second bad decision can bring upon families."

He pauses for a moment, then shifts his focus to me. "He is a trusted voice in our community, bringing us the news with integrity and dedication. You know him well; you welcome him into your homes at dinnertime. And before you turn on the news to hear of yet another tragedy that has bloodied the streets of Los Angeles, he hears of it first. He investigates, uncovers the truth, and delivers it to you with all of the shocking details." It's my turn to smile and nod in acknowledgement. "Together, they are a beautiful couple, partnering to play a pivotal role in our organization's success and drive critical change in legislation, with your help. Please welcome Amanda and Paul Davis, ladies and gentlemen!"

My wife and I stand as the audience starts applauding. Beaming, Carly chooses that moment to step up into our limelight and hug me, as if we're at the Oscars or something. She lingers in the hug, filling my nostrils with her scent, grinding her hip against me. I pull away discreetly, knowing all cameras are trained on us. Then, I offer Amanda an arm that she quickly takes as we walk toward the makeshift stage.

She stands by my side at the lectern when I take the mic. The crowd quiets down looking at me, and I love it. "Thank you all for being here tonight. Before we get into the serious stuff, I wanted to share a little joke I heard recently: Why did the reporter sit on the teleprompter?" A pause for effect. "Because they wanted to stay on top of the news!"

The audience laughs heartily, and I bask in it. Then, as the response subsides, I continue. "Alright, now that we've had a laugh, let me tell you a story." I look at my wife, and she nods almost imperceptibly. "About how we started *Citizens Against Impaired Driving*, and, most of all, why. It was when we both realized that our jobs had too much death in them. For Amanda, it was the lives that the amazing team at Sunset Valley couldn't save. Senseless deaths that could've been avoided. For me, it was the litany of incidents I had to bring to you via the news I delivered, every single night. Not a day of respite in our lives and yours; not a day of not having to talk about yet another horrifying 'accident' happening here in LA." I allow a beat of silence to pass so my message can sink in. "It just has to stop. And you can make it happen. *We* can make it happen. Together."

As I say those words, the last of them being drowned by enthusiastic applause, my throat scorches for a drink. At a table close to the podium, the beauty in the backless red dress smiles at me.

I make eye contact and hold it for a moment. Her smile blooms, her head tilting slightly as she throws me a loaded look.

For a moment, I forget about Amanda.

Who knows what the evening might still bring? It's looking good for now.

Like *A Beautiful Couple?*

Buy it now!

ABOUT THE AUTHOR

Meet Leslie Wolfe, bestselling author and mastermind behind gripping thrillers that have won the hearts of over three million readers worldwide. She brings a fresh and invigorating touch to the thriller genre, crafting compelling narratives around unforgettable, powerhouse women.

You might know her from the Detective Kay Sharp series or have been hooked by Tess Winnett's relentless pursuit of justice. Maybe you've followed the dynamic duo Baxter & Holt through the gritty streets of Las Vegas or plunged into political intrigue with Alex Hoffmann.

Recently, Leslie published *The Girl You Killed*, a psychological thriller that's pure, unputdownable suspense. This standalone novel will have fans of *The Undoing*, *The Silent Patient*, and *Little Fires Everywhere* on the edge of their seats.

Whether you're into the mind games of *Criminal Minds*, love crime thrillers like James Patterson's, or enjoy the heart-pounding tension in Kendra Elliot and Robert Dugoni's mysteries, Leslie's got a thriller series for you. Fans of action-packed writers like Tom Clancy or Lee Child will find plenty to love in her Alex Hoffmann series.

Wolfe's latest psychological thriller, *A Beautiful Couple*, will have you racing through the pages gasping for breath until the final jaw-dropping twist, delighting fans of *Gone Girl* and *The Girl on the Train*.

Discover all of Leslie's works on Amazon.com/LeslieWolfe. Want a sneak peek at what's next? Become an insider for early access to previews of her new novels, each a thrilling ride you won't want to miss.

BOOKS BY LESLIE WOLFE

STANDALONE TITLES

A Beautiful Couple
The Surgeon
The Girl You Killed
The Hospital
If I Go Missing
Stories Untold
Love, Lies and Murder

TESS WINNETT SERIES

Dawn Girl
The Watson Girl
Glimpse of Death
Taker of Lives
Not Really Dead
Girl With A Rose
Mile High Death
The Girl They Took
The Girl Hunter

DETECTIVE KAY SHARP SERIES

The Girl From Silent Lake
Beneath Blackwater River
The Angel Creek Girls
The Girl on Wildfire Ridge
Missing Girl at Frozen Falls

BAXTER & HOLT SERIES

Las Vegas Girl
Casino Girl
Las Vegas Crime

ALEX HOFFMANN SERIES

Executive
Devil's Move
The Backup Asset
The Ghost Pattern
Operation Sunset

For the complete list of books in all available formats, visit:
Amazon.com/LeslieWolfe